BOUNTY MAN AND DOE

Bounty Man and Doe

Dusty Richards

THORNDIKE PRESS
A part of Gale, a Cengage Company

Thorndike Press® Large Print Softcover Western.
The text of this Large Print edition is unabridged.
Other aspects of the book may vary from the original edition.
Set in 16 pt. Plantin.

LIBRARY OF CONGRESS CIP DATA ON FILE.
CATALOGUING IN PUBLICATION FOR THIS BOOK
IS AVAILABLE FROM THE LIBRARY OF CONGRESS.

ISBN-13: 978-1-4205-1927-3 (softcover alk. paper)

Published in 2024 by arrangement with Roan & Weatherford Publishing Associates.

This one's for Amy

FOREWORD

I had heard about Dusty Richards long before I met him. Family and friends knew him from radio broadcasts and writing presentations . . . and for his western novels, of course. My first impression of Dusty when I met him was that he was a blustery kind of guy — and he was, but for whatever reason, we got along straight away. Maybe it was because we both graduated from Arizona State, though years apart. Dusty sure liked to tell his stories — and there were plenty of them — and I sure liked to hear them.

We were at many author meetings together and I always enjoyed seeing Dusty and visiting with him. He was always working at these gatherings, with his laptop right in front of him, banging out another of his limitless supply of books. Oh, they needed editing all right, but he could turn out a western faster than you could believe — and successful ones, too. One of the greatest honors of my life was serving as an historical advisor and beta reader on a few of those stories, including one that would become the novel Zekial. Dusty was so appreciative of my help, he even named a character after me, a colorful trapper and frontiersman named "Whistling Dick" Hogan.

Dusty Richards was a blast of a guy and a heckuva western writer. His readers loved him and he loved them, answering every email, letter, or request. He was just that kind of guy. His loss is still deeply felt by his many fans and friends alike, and we won't soon forget him. And we don't have to — he saw to that, leaving a cupboard full of tales yet to be printed.

Thanks, Dusty, we'll always remember you, pal.

— J.B. Hogan
Fayetteville, Arkansas
February 28, 2020

PROLOGUE

The conversation around the poker table centered mostly on places they'd been and men they'd known. Bill Hickock, Bass Reeves, and Chris Madsen were mentioned. Someone asked Doc if he'd ever heard of a bounty man called Brennen.

"Why sure," Holliday said in his soft Georgia drawl. "I knew Sam Brennen. I'll see your two bits and raise ya four more, I recollect he worked a spell as a deputy for Wyatt back in Wichita." The poker playing dentist wiped the sweat from his brow while studying the other card players around the table in the Birdcage Theater that warm afternoon. "He's a quiet, peaceful enough man. In Wichita, he married a Dutch woman who had two children."

"I heard he was a town-taming marshal," one of the players said.

"Where was it, Sam got that town marshal job?" Doc asked himself absently. Then, as

9

if he recalled, he shook his head to continue. "I recall it was some mining camp up in Colorado."

"I'll raise you four more," said Judge Spicer.

"It's a sorry day when an honest gambler can't even buy a pot." Doc folded his cards in disgust. "Someone said a bunch of drunk miners killed his whole family while he was gone."

"Whose family, John?" Spicer asked.

"Sam Brennan's," Doc replied. "Pretty gory deal."

"What happened then?" one of the players asked.

"Nobody knows, but I heard that he's bounty hunting now with some mean squaw." Doc twisted in his chair. "Wyatt?"

"What's that Doc?" the Marshal asked from the bar.

"Where did Sam get that gun totin' Injun bitch rides with him?"

"Search me."

"She as mean as they say, Wyatt?"

"Well, them two rounded up a bunch of stage robbers in Colorado. Heard she blew one old boy to hell an' gone with a shotgun for reaching for his gun." Wyatt said with a shake of his head. "She must be tough enough."

"I heard that she was Natise's daughter," said Doc.

"Who knows who she is, but Sam Brennen has her riding along with him. I guess he's got him a helluva outfit to collect them rewards," Wyatt said, leaning back with his elbows on top of the bar.

Doc agreed then broke into coughing that he finally suppressed with a straight shot of whiskey before he spoke again. "He keeps on the move. Must still be looking for those old boys that kilt his family." Doc began studying his new hand.

"You reckon he's still doing that?" a player asked across the table.

"Can't be sure, but if determination and an Indian squaw will help, I'd hate to be the ones he thought had done it," Holliday said and folded.

"Doc, I'm going down to the OK Corral and check on my horse. He's still lame," Wyatt said, finishing his drink.

"Well by gawd, take these damn flies down there with you!"

"Them flies bringing you bad luck?" Earp frowned and acted amused.

"Ain't won a damned hand all afternoon."

Wyatt smiled and shook his head as he started for the front door. Under the shaded porch, he could still hear Doc coughing as he crossed the street. Where in the hell was Sam Brennen anyway?

CHAPTER No. 1

Sam searched the diggings from Fort Collins to south of Denver for the men who had killed his wife and stepdaughters. Bearded men in the night, no clues, his family's blood all over the rooms. Two or three men in a mean stupor of alcohol had destroyed a dream. They ended the tranquil domicile where he escaped the pressures of the badge. Charged with the job of protecting the entire community, he had failed his own. As the search became more and more futile, he began to really drink.

Whiskey helped him numb the hopelessness as one day ran into the next one. His guts churned as he rode the day, at last deciding through his booze fogged mind, he was lost.

The bay horse picked its way up the stream-laced canyon. There was something ahead. A blurred figure was beating a pile of hides or something on it. His eyes would not focus.

"Hello, the camp," he said, reining the horse up.

"Move on, mister. I ain't got no time for saddle bums."

"What you beating on there?"

"None of your damn business! You whup your squaw, by gawd, and I'll whup mine!"

He was a bearded man in buckskin, big as a grizzly and just as dirty, and armed with a large quirt.

Sam squinted, trying to see. "Are you whipping a woman?"

"This here is *my* squaw, mister. I aim to whup her 'til she learns a lesson."

"Get back!" Sam ordered, dismounting.

"Nobody tells me what to do in my own damn camp. Now, you git."

"I'm telling you. Stop whipping that woman."

"You better fill your hand, bushwhacker!" The whiskered man grabbed for the barking iron in his waistband. The bay horse bolted in front of Sam. The bullets from the other man's gun struck the animal and he reared in pain.

With the reaction of a man familiar with a gun, Brennen's fist filled with his Colt as he moved clear of his dying mount. He emptied the .45 into the surprised man's body. Each slug hit with a *thud* and fountain of blood as they spun him around and sent him crashing to the ground.

Balancing unsteadily on his boot heels, Sam saw the fearful dark eyes of the girl. She was hardly more than a teenager.

Turning, she watched her twisting, dying tormentor as he gurgled his last blasphemous moments on earth. Then she surveyed the tottering stranger, busy reloading his pistol and spilling cartridges on the ground. She prepared to meet her ancestors.

"You got any coffee?" He leaned over her. "Well . . . you have any coffee?"

Swallowing hard, she nodded and scurried off on all fours to obey. Returning quickly, she held a steaming metal cup in her hands with her head bowed obediently.

The cup instantly began to burn his palms. Setting it down on a rock, he wondered how she had even brought it to him. Rubbing his stinging palm, he studied her carefully. In her worn buckskins, she waited for her destiny, head bowed.

"Who is he?" Sam asked, puzzled. Perhaps she did not understand English. "Who *was* he, I mean?"

Trembling, she rose to stand before him, but still did not speak. Shrugging his shoulders, he tried the coffee again — it was cooling. The bitter vapors helped clear his head but still burnt his throat going down. He gagged and choked, the sour taste flooding his mouth. His body jerked over forward, convulsing as he threw up. He heaved and heaved again. Finally, when nothing else came forth, he had the dry convulsions that followed. Swirling his brain into semi-darkness, he fought the loss of consciousness.

"Damn it, girl! Who is this crazy nut that shot my horse?" He coughed, half-rising on his knees as she offered him a drink of water. Swallowing hard, he pointed with the canteen at the now-stiffening corpse.

Her eyes blazed with anger. "Him, Joe Sunday!"

"Joe Sunday, huh? Don't reckon that means much to me. Who are you?"

"Doe."

He cocked his right eye open. "Doe who?"

"Doe," she said again. Pointing to herself, she raised her shoulders with the dignity of royalty. "My name. Doe."

"Sam Brennen" he said, pointing at himself with the canteen.

Doe turned and spat on her late tormentor, kicking him with a bare brown foot. "Bad man! Good he is gone to spirits."

"Right, now we better bury your ex-

16

husband — owner, whatever — and figure what the hell to do next."

"No. You eat. Plenty time to bury him." She passed him a plate of steaming stew. "You skinny."

He sniffed it cautiously, testing his senses and his stomach. He decided it might stay down. She was right. He couldn't think of when he'd eaten last. His belly told him it had been a while, though.

The stew needed salt, but Sam resisted the urge to mention it. At least it settled on his shaky stomach. He looked her over as he ate. Her nose was narrow and had been broken at some point in the recent past, maybe by that rattler he'd shot. Her eyes were deep, dark brown pools under the longest lashes he'd ever seen. She was a bit on the short side, but her body was well-proportioned with youthful curves. Put all that together with skin the color of tanned leather, she was an Indian for sure, but he couldn't easily tell her tribe. Out here, she could be Sioux, Cheyenne, or who knew what else.

Enough about her looks, he reminded himself. He wasn't interested in her as an object. If he'd been out in the diggings for a season, he wouldn't have culled much of anything female.

17

Smoke from the fire changed its direction, and he looked up. She was not eating, watching him across the fire as if awaiting some command. Rising, she came around and refilled his coffee cup.

He pointed. "You eat!"

She shook her head and grinned, seemingly pleased with him.

"Get some food and sit down over here." He patted a place beside him for her to come sit by him. "I've a million questions to ask you."

With a shrug, she filled a bowl and sat down on his side of the fire, cross-legged. He swallowed, trying hard not to notice her bare brown knees and shapely legs obvious. "Where are your people?"

"No people." She scooped the stew up with her fingers, raised them to her mouth, and began licking them delicately.

"What tribe do you belong to?"

"No tribe. Belong to Joe Sunday. No more Sunday." She pointed at him. "Now belong to Sam."

"No. Hell, no. We're taking you home to your people."

"They cut my nose off!" She made a knife-like motion across her face, her voice turning fearful.

"Okay. There are some problems that

can't be solved tonight," Sam admitted, shaking his head. "Is there a shovel?"

"Find one after you eat."

He shrugged. "I guess."

Searching through the panniers after they ate, he found a short-handled shovel and used it to test the sandy creek bottom. Patting him on the arm, she stopped him. Taking the shovel away, she shook her head at him and began digging the grave herself.

Darkness was filling the canyon as Sam searched the dead man. Stripping the ammunition belt off the body, he placed it with the man's old black powder pistol. There were several gold Mexican coins in a leather pouch from around his neck, with even more in the panniers and several ounces of gold dust in a chamois pouch. No papers identified him as Joe Sunday, only her word. He must have been about fortyish, Sam judged, and had seen some hard living. Left index finger gone. Big knife scars on his forearm from some kind of bad fight.

Grabbing the corpse beneath the arms and struggling hard, Sam lifted it off the ground and drug it over to the hole Doe was preparing. The bandit was so heavy, he considered getting a horse and a rope for the task, but decided against it. Finally, now sweating and out of breath, he managed to manhandle the body over to the hole. Finding a tattered trading blanket under the panniers, he wrapped the remains up in it.

Doe looked up from the bottom of the shallow pit, displeasure written all over her face. "Joe Sunday not worth old blanket!"

"Your opinion, but even he deserves a Christian burial." He motioned her out of the hole. "I think that's deep enough."

Still grumbling, she pulled herself up and over the lip of the grave. In the short time he'd been occupied with the body, she'd managed to dig out about three feet.

Puffing mightily, Sam strained against the body again, rolling it into over and into the hole.

With a shrug of her shoulders, Doe spat upon Sunday one last time, and began covering the body with dirt.

"Wait." He stopped her, taking the shovel. Pulling off his hat, Sam held it in his hand and cleared his throat. "Lord, we're delivering this sinner to Your grace and —"

She didn't let him finish.

"Give me damn shovel." She snatched the implement from him.

"Stop it, Doe!"

They tussled over the tool for a moment before he finally wrested it from her calloused fingers.

"Doe go clean dishes." She stomped off barefooted, back to the fire.

"Lord help me." He shook his head, looking up at the star-flecked sky. "I don't even know where I'm at. My horse is dead, this wild bear of a man is dead, and now I've some Indian girl on my hands, too. Are you trying to tell me something here?"

Silence. Apparently the Good Lord wasn't answering prayers tonight. With a sigh, he went back to filling the grave.

Later, when he'd finished the burial, he walked slowly back to the fire and sat down. Doe was scrubbing the dishes in a steamy kettle.

"More food?"

He shook his head. He wasn't hungry anymore. What he really needed was to know more about her. "Where did you hook up with Joe Sunday?"

"At a river. He paid two men some gold for me."

"What river?"

"I was never there before. They called it the Rio Bravo.

He nodded. That meant Texas or New Mexico Territory, most likely. "Where did you learn English?"

"Mission. Priest teach me English. How to read and write. Learn much at mission."

Good. That gave him a lead on where to take her back to, at least. A priest wouldn't cut off her nose. "You lived by a mission?"

"We lived in mountains with our people." She shrugged. "One day, Peralta brothers came and killed my mother. Mean men. Bad men. They scalped her. They stole my brother and me. They use me like a woman, many times. At a place of dirt houses, they sold us to another mean man. He beat us and we not know why. All time he beat us. The *padre* take us to mission. No more bad food, no more bad barn to sleep in. *Padre* teach us English and pray to his Jesus. Brother run away to ride with Natise. He not like Papago at mission. He is warrior.

"One day I decided to run away to my people. I am not a good woman. My life spoiled by the men who kill my mother.

"So, I wandered alone until two men on mules take me with them. Not too mean to me, but they sell me to no good Joe Sunday for gold. He ride back trails, go to Colorado, find more gold. No stop in towns, he mad all the time. Beat Doe 'cause he mad. Then Sam come."

Sam coughed, and his cheeks grew hot. He studied the buckskin-clad girl-woman sitting cross-legged beside him. He thought of the trials she'd been drug through, the

22

indignities she'd suffered.

She broke his chain of thought. "You know my story?"

"I do. It's sad." He swallowed and looked into the fire, unable to meet her eyes for some reason. "I'm sorry for what you've been through."

"What your story."

Sam bit his lip. "Some outlaws killed my wife and two daughters a while back. I've been searching the gold camps for them ever since. You know the men who hurt you. That's something, at least. All I know about the men who killed my family is they are miners." His voice broke, and he cleared his throat. "Hell, I've been looking for ghosts for months. I don't even know where we're at right now."

"You lose all your family?"

"Yes. But you don't understand. They are gone like smoke. Like ghosts."

"I help you find these men, then we ride, and we get Peralta brothers?"

He held his palms out. "How in the world can we find ghosts?"

"No ghosts kill your wife. They leave a trail, you miss sign. Need good Indian to find the way. Need Doe. Then we'll go find the Peraltas."

"Let's sleep on it. I've done enough thinking for one day."

"You want me sleep with you?"

It was a flat matter-of-fact statement that made him cringe. He had not even considered sleeping with another woman since burying his wife. "No, not tonight."

She frowned. "You not ride off and leave Doe?"

"No." He turned an ear to a lone wolf howling up on the mountain above. The sound made Sunday's horses shuffle with unease, but they were hobbled. In a few moments, the lonely, hair-raising cry was answered by several more.

Sam shivered.

She laughed, rubbing her chilled arms. "Doe build up fire, so wolves don't come eat us. Be too cold to sleep alone."

He ignored her offer. "Yah, okay."

Getting his bedroll from his dead horse, he dropped into his blankets, snuggling down into their warmth with his pistol in hand. Peeking out above the covers, he watched her churn up the fire. Sparks flying blindly, she poked it with a vengeance and sat down to stare into the flames.

What the hell was he going to do with her?

CHAPTER No. 2

The golden globe of dawn had filtered over the eastern mountain when the clang of a Dutch oven lid woke him. For a moment, he forgot where he was and what had happened the day before. He smelled fresh bread, boiling coffee, and campfire smoke. It was almost like he was back home, with Agnes and the girls.

But then it all came rushing back.

Damn it.

Doe noticed him moving under the blankets. "Good morning."

"Morning." He threw the blankets off, stood, and stretched the stiffness in his back.

"You not ride off and leave Doe. You good man." She heaped bread and beans into a tin bowl. "Where we go first, Sam?"

He considered this for a moment. "These horses look like they need a week of good grass. We have enough food to stay here?"

"Enough food. Plenty of grass for horses."

"What else we got?"

"Not know." She shrugged and jerked her head toward the packs. "Look after breakfast."

Well, he couldn't argue with that. How long had it been since he had eaten fresh bread, anyway? Sam took the bowl and a steaming cup of coffee. Savoring the food, he leaned his shoulder against a pine tree. Doe sat across from him, eating from her own bowl and studying him silently.

Trying to ignore her gaze, he turned his glance to the pack saddles and their gear. What was in them he had not found? Had the old man had anything besides the gold and the coins he'd found the night before? Finishing his meal, he wiped his mouth on his sleeve. The stale smell of trail dust and horse burnt his nose. He needed to do some laundry soon.

He set the plate down on a nearby rock and dug into the packs. A moment later, he grinned like a fool, having found several cans of peaches Joe Sunday had stashed under some ragged shirts. The old bastard had been holding out on them, after all.

Among the food and other plunder he found some papers, too. Pulling them out, he studied them intently. There was a filed mining claim in Yavapai County, Arizona Territory, for mineral, along with a rich assay report on some ore. There was a wanted poster, as well, for a stage robber, named Joe Molloy. The description fit Sunday's bill right down to the missing finger. Looking at the dates, the claim was a year old, and the poster was three.

"Find big secret?"

Sam nodded. "His name is Joe Molloy. He was a stage robber — there's a reward out on him."

"Much money?"

"Fifty dollars." He shrugged. "If we're going to search for the Peralta brothers, we'll need some money. Besides, the old outlaw owes us that much for shooting my horse."

"Good!" She clapped her hands, grinning widely. "Horses get fat. We go find them."

"Can you shoot a gun?"

"Never shoot gun, but Doe can learn faster than horses can get fat."

He studied her face, wondering if he was doing the right thing. Lord knew he could use some help tracking down the bandits that had killed Agnes and their girls. Just look where his lousy tracking skills had gotten him so far.

But if he went through with this, he would be honor-bound to help her track down her tormentors, as well . . . no matter where they may be.

Well, hell. What else was he going to do?

Finally, with a shrug, he swept up Joe's pistol and motioned for her to follow. Excited as a school girl, she practically ran to keep up with him as he led the way out into the brush to find a spot for a shooting lesson.

Studying him carefully as he took aim, Doe watched the big gray rock on the slope he'd pointed out for her to see it hit.

The report of the pistol echoed up and down the valley, spooking the horses from their grazing. A piece of rock flew in the air as the bullet found its mark.

Sam handed her the pistol. It was huge in her little hands, and her arms trembled trying to keep it steady. He tried to help her hold it, instructing her on how to aim. She pulled the trigger and the pistol bucked, rocking her entire body backward. When the smoked cleared, the rock that was their target was still intact. The ball had obviously gone wild. But his student was determined, and was soon firing the heavy revolver all by herself.

Sam leaned against a nearby aspen and watched as she reloaded the gun with fierce, unwavering concentration. By the third shot, she was sending pieces of rock flying. When she emptied the gun again, she threw her head back and gazed up at him with a look of immense pride. "I tell you."

"Yes, you did. I think you need a smaller gun, but you're learning, alright." He laughed as she leaped into his arms and hugged him tightly. "Hey, now. No need for all that. You did a good job."

She suddenly realized what she was doing. With wide eyes — almost terrified — she jerked back, cowering, dropping the heavy revolver in the process.

The silence of the morning stretched out around them, broken only by the sound of a few singing birds.

Sam swallowed. "Doe, why are you afraid?"

"You no want touch. Doe forget. Maybe you hit —"

He didn't let her finish.

"No, I won't. That's not something you have to worry about." He took hold of her shoulders. "You are a good student, too. But be more careful, okay? That gun can kill you or me."

She nodded. "Doe is careful. No great thing to shoot gun."

"Well, you do learn fast. Maybe we can shoot some more tomorrow."

"No." She picked the revolver back up, the incident of a moment before seemingly forgotten. She admired the rust-pitted barrel. "Shoot more now, get better."

The sun was warming up the timber-clad slopes when Sam slipped off to the nearby mountain stream. He needed a bath as well as some clean clothes. Stripping down to his underwear, he stood in the cold water to his knees and soaked his shirt and cord pants. He was so intent on his task, he did not hear Doe come up behind him.

"You are poor squaw, Sam. Take off clothes. I will clean."

He looked at her over his shoulder. "You can wash clothes?"

"I learn much at mission. Get clothes off."

"Um . . ." His cheeks heated up again. What was it about this woman that made him blush like a little girl? "After I get a blanket."

"You are strange man." She shook her head in disbelief as he scampered off back to the campsite. Returning a minute later wrapped in a rough blanket, he took off his underwear and threw them to her.

Sitting in the warm sun, he watched her with fascination. She washed the clothes with yucca roots she had gathered, and the suds swirled off in rivulets over the shoal. Finishing with his clothes, she laid them on some nearby rocks to dry, and without a word, slipped out of her own buckskin dress. She stepped lithely stepped into the stream and soon was lathering her smooth, brown skin with the soap.

Sam turned away, watching a hawk riding the updrafts far above so as to avoid gazing upon her nudity. He leaned against the cottonwood and shook his head tried to take his mind — and his eyes — off her toned, shapely body. Finely, she wrung out her long, black hair and sat down to sun herself beside the stream as her copper brown skin dried. After what seemed like an eternity, she picked up her wash-worn faded dress, held it over her head, and wiggled into it.

She smoothed the buckskin stretched across her ample bosom. "I will go so you can bathe."

"Thanks," he muttered, embarrassed, and relieved to be left alone at last.

Dropping the blanket, he crossed the sharp rocks and scampered gingerly into the stream.

He never noticed Doe watching him from the bushes.

Doe laughed quietly to herself as she

watched, pleased with what she saw. "He is big man."

After a few minutes, she turned away and whistled her way back to camp and began cleaning up and gathering wood for the fire. Soon he would be back, this strange white man who grew red at the sight of her skin. He must be thinking of his murdered wife. That made him good man. She would do as he asked for now, and keep her distance. There was still much sorrow inside him. That would change, though. Someday he would see that she was a woman, too.

She would care for him, she decided, until he was ready to live again.

After a week, they left the place Sam had come to call Dead Horse Canyon. Riding a roman-nosed gray, he led the way while Doe rode proudly behind them on a small bay that bore a crude Y-brand. Across her lap, a double-barrel shotgun glistened with oil in the sun. Her bare legs shone in the sunlight as she brought up the train.

Camped at the foot of the mountains that night, Sam recognized enough local landmarks to finally figure out where they were and orient their line of travel accordingly. The next day they rode into Johnson Camp, a tent city set up to supply the area's gold hunters.

Leaving Doe with the horses, he marched into the largest tent, a dingy affair marked as "Sally's." The floor was sawdust, and the air reeked of sour booze, smoke, and cheap perfume.

A white-shirted faro operator with his sleeves tied up with garters beckoned him over to the corner table. Sam shook his head and bellied up to the bar, instead.

"What'll it be?" the handlebar-mustached barkeeper asked.

"Beer."

"You don't look like a miner, mister."

Pushing his hat back on his head, Sam scanned the thin crowd casually. "Can't always tell a book by the cover."

"That's what I say — sometimes, at least. Hey, are you lonely? I can get you a girl if you are so inclined, Mister. . . ."

"Just Sam."

"Proud to meet you, Just Sam. I'm Jack." They shook hands. "So what do you say about that girl?"

Studying the foamy mug intently, Sam caught the barmen motioning to someone behind him. He stiffened and glanced up at the mirror behind the bar. Old habits die hard, he guessed. No threat — just a pretty soiled dove in a red dress swaying his way.

Jack was the joint's barkeep and pimp, apparently. Nice arrangement.

"Nah, I'm good for now. Just need a beer to wash off the trail dust. You know how it is."

Jack nodded. Frowning in disappointment, he waved the girl away. His tone was slightly less solicitous when he spoke again. "Anything else?"

"Actually, yeah, there is. I'm looking for three guys. An outfit I used to work with. Would've showed up here three, maybe four months ago. One of 'em is real handy with a knife. Seen anybody like that?"

"Mister, that could be any one of hundreds. They come and go like jackrabbits here."

"Worth a shot, at least." Sam shrugged and finished the beer in one long pull. "I'll be around for a few days if you think of something, though."

"How do I get hold of you?"

"Oh, don't worry." With a lopsided grin, Sam slapped a quick tattoo on the wood of the bar and winked. "I'll be around."

"Sure thing."

Turning to leave, Sam saw a grubby old miner with a ragged beard further down the bar nudge his companion. "Hey, I think I seen that guy somewhere before. Who is he?"

"Not so loud." The second miner shushed the man. "That's Brennen. He used to be Marshal up at Fort Collins. What I want to know is why you reckon that squaw of his is out there drawing a crowd?"

"Damned if I know."

Sam slowed. A squaw drawing a crowd? What the hell — ?

That's when the gunshot cut the air outside.

Doe!

Adrenaline surging through his veins, Sam pulled his Colt and rushed out the entrance into the muddy street. Doe stood where he'd left her beside their horses, only now with her revolver drawn and smoking. Two more dirty miners — you could hardly tell them apart they were all so filthy — were on the ground, pleading with her not to shoot them.

He gritted his teeth and marched toward the pair through the ankle-deep mud, pistol up and cocked. "You two! Yeah, you! Get the hell away from her."

"We didn't mean nothin' by it, mister, I swear!"

"We just thought she was purty!"

"Up!" Sam jerked the barrel of the pistol.

"Get up and get out of here before I let her shoot you in the ass!"

Both now covered in grime, they clamored to their feet and ran.

The curious crowd began to melt away. Sam holstered his revolver and went over to stand beside Doe.

She tucked the pistol back into the Joe Sunday's old holster. "You mad?"

"Did you have to draw that kind of attention?"

"They want to know where I get these horses. They want me to get in bed." The look in her dark eyes made him think of nothing but a murderous, angry eagle. "They tell me to fuck them and do something with my mouth."

Sam sighed. He'd have done the same damn thing in her situation. "He was asking you something that wasn't to be asked. You did the right thing."

"Whiskey make men crazy." She shook her head.

"Can't argue with that." He spied a spent case on the ground and bent to pick it up. It was one of hers. At least she had reloaded. "Let's get out of here, huh? We need to find us a camp and check some things out."

They made camp under a grove of cottonwoods beside a small stream a little ways

36

outside of town. Doe set about building a fire out of what little she could find — a mixture of dried cow chips from a nearby pasture and a few pieces of dry driftwood. It smelled horrible and attracted a cloud of buzzing black flies. Sam tried to bed down for a nap in the shade, but the combination of insects, heat, and the ungodly stench forced him to abandon that idea.

From under the brim of his hat, he watched his new companion go about her business of setting up their campsite. She had a boundless, restless energy to her. A strength of will that was almost physical. More than that, with her dark eyes, lustrous black hair, and perfect legs, she was beautiful. No wonder those miners had wanted to take her out for a roll in the hay.

The miners. Dirty old bastards. Even the thought of them made him want to strangle someone. He studied her again. Yeah, no wonder they'd propositioned her. In those ragged old buckskins ol' Joe had kept her in, she looked like a squaw ready to be sold like a horse at auction. He needed to do something about that. And sooner rather than later.

Rising with a sigh, he pulled on his gun-belt and buckled it.

Doe looked up from stoking the campfire,

her brow furrowing. "Where you go?"

"Back into town for a little while." He saddled up the gray, swung aboard, and tipped the brim of his hat. "Don't worry, I'll be back soon."

"You promise?"

Sam grinned. She was like a little girl sometimes. "I promise."

Dismounting in front of the tent marked "General Store," Sam hitched the gray to the rail. Stepping inside, he nodded to an eager young clerk who rushed forward to wait on him.

"Can I help you, mister?"

"Yes, you certainly can. Do you stock clothes for women around here?"

The youth nodded. "Yes, sir, we surely do. Right over this way."

Sam picked his way through the various shelves and racks stacked neatly with skirts, blouses, and all manner of other clothing.

He searched through the stacks of canvas pants, estimating Doe's waist size to be sure to find something that would fit her. He picked a gray wool skirt that she could tie around her waist. There was a blue blouse with ruffles that caught his eye, and he held it out in front of himself, hoping it would be the right size.

Off the rack, in the rear, he chose a long boy's jacket made from a trade blanket. It was a striped coat of white, blue, and red. Finally, he picked up a gray, unblocked hat and added it to the pile.

Satisfied, he took it all up front, where the clerk bundled and tied it all up and the older storekeeper gave added up the total purchase. Sam paid the man, leaving a tip for the youngster's help, and headed back to camp.

Reining up, Sam grinned. The young clerk had bundled everything up but the hat, so he grabbed it and sailed it through the air and into Doe's surprised arms. "What is this?"

"It's for you. I figured you needed something to wear besides that rag of a dress and that old buckskin outfit." He laughed as she clapped it on her head modeled it in various positions.

Sam dismounted, untied each of the bundles from the saddle, and handed them to her. He watched as she pulled the strings and the clothes came spilling out. She held them up one at a time to examine them, an expression of awe on her face — pants, skirt, blouses, gloves . . . Last but not least, the blanket jacket slipped out and fell to the ground. She recovered it in an instant, care-

39

fully brushing dry grass and dirt from the fabric.

"Here!" Laughing, Doe handed him the coat and wiggled the buckskin dress over her head. She wore nothing beneath it. Sam's face flamed and he was certain he'd turned beet red. He looked away as she hurriedly pulled on the pants and grabbed one of the blouses from a nearby rock. In an instant, she took the skirt and tied it around her waist.

When he looked back her way, she was fully dressed again, with her hat cocked jauntily to one side, whirling around like a dancer for his inspection. Her joy was infectious.

Sam began to laugh, and did so until tears rolled down his cheeks.

She stopped her twirling, looking up at him in confusion. "What's wrong, Sam Brennen?"

"Nothing. Nothing." He shook his head and wiped his face with a sleeve. "You just look . . . different. That's all."

"Am I not pretty?"

"You're more than simply pretty, Doe. Trust me, you're beautiful. Now more than ever."

Her expression brightened, and she rushed into his arms. This time, he held her as tightly as she did him.

"Thank you for my new clothes, Sam. You good man."

"You're welcome. You're a good woman yourself, Doe."

Holding one another, they stood together in the golden afternoon sun, content. When it became increasingly obvious how much they were both enjoying themselves, though, Sam broke gingerly away and held her at arm's length. He had to be careful. If he let this beautiful girl-women in too far. . . .

He cleared his throat. "Doe, tonight, I'm going back into town to check things out and see if I can learn anything."

"I go?"

"No, I don't want you hurt. Those miners are crazy about Indian women. They figure that squaws are all fair game, and you're as pretty as they come."

"No!" She didn't take that well at all. "We find men who kill your wife. Together. Doe take care of herself."

"I said no."

She wasn't through with her argument, though. Stomping her foot, she brought herself to her full height and fixed him with a steely gaze. "I say yes. I wrap up in old blanket, they think I am old, dirty squaw. No one will want me. You see, Sam."

41

Lord, this woman was a handful. He kicked a nearby pile of horse manure. "I don't like it."

"I no like stay here even more."

He looked sideways at her, standing there by the fire, her mouth set and her fist on her hip, full of defiance. What on earth was he going to do with her?

"Aww, hell," he said finally. "Okay, you can go spying with me tonight."

Chapter No. 3

The town was beginning to come alive as he dismounted at the hitch rack. Sounds of a tinny piano in Sally's filtered into the crowded street. Slipping inside, he moved to the bar, observing the customers, and ordered a beer. Excited gamblers shouted as lady luck came their way or eluded them.

Typical night of win or lose in a mining camp.

Doe left the bay in a shallow wash on the outskirts of town, stealing her way slowly and carefully through the narrow back streets. She listened to the activity around her, trying to avoid as many people as possible. A dog barked at her from a space between two tents, but he was no threat to her. A little further on, she stubbed her toe on a glass bottle lying in the mud. Slumping down behind a stack of empty crates, she hunkered down beneath the tattered blanket. There was still some liquor at the bottom of the container, and it gave her an idea. She poured some over her greased-down, matted hair, then rubbed more of the burning liquid on her face. She was sure to stink like the rest of the back-alley whores now.

Doe was about to to drop the bottle and move on when the sound of harsh voices from down the alley reached her ears. A trio of men were stumbling down the alley toward her, talking loudly. She froze in place, afraid to even breathe.

"It's him, I tell ya," one of them said. "I swear, it's Sam Brennen!"

The mention of Sam's name shocked her. Who were these men? And how did they know Sam?

"Are you sure?" a second man asked.

"Hell, yeah, I'm sure. Didn't you see him back in the bar? We're lucky he didn't see us. He's looking for us. Everywhere we go, he comes, too."

A third voice, deeper, more masculine, obviously the leader of the group, sounded bored. "He don't know who we are. There'd be bounty posters out if'n he did."

The first man wasn't having it, though. "Listen here, Cal. I don't aim for him to figure it out."

"Lower your damn voice, Digger. We can

44

handle him."

"No way. I'm for getting the hell out of here!"

"Lawd, Digger, shut *up*. We need to get our stuff at the claim and figure out what to *do*."

"But —"

"But nothin'. Shut yer trap a'fore I have to clean your plow." The leader chuffed the first man across the back of the head. "Now come on, stupid,"

Her heart pounding, Doe clutched her knees under her chin and crouched behind the splintered crates as one of them bumped into the pile. An eternity seemed to passed as she listened to their fading footsteps through the mud and muck.

When she was sure they were gone, she slipped out of her hiding place and, hugging the blanket to her, stumbled out of the shadows. Hurrying back to her horse with this newfound bit of information, she nearly ran into two drunks coming around the corner of a broke-down carryall.

"Hey! Come have a drink, darlin'."

Shaking her head, she pushed on, ignoring the offer. When they started to pursue, she broke into a run.

"Aww, hell with you," one of them shouted after her. "Dirty squaw! You smell like shit, anyway!"

Swinging onto the bay in one smooth motion, she loped the horse off into the night, tears streaming down her cheeks. She'd just stumbled on to the killers of Sam's family. Doe *knew* it, could smell it on them. Yet the knowledge terrified her. She and Sam had just started to form a real connection, one unlike she'd ever experienced before. If they found and dealt with the killers he was seeking, would he keep his promise to come with her back to Arizona to find the Peralta brothers? Or would he simply ride off one night and leave her to her fate? She thought about the possibilities all the way back to camp.

Jumping off the bay, she stripped off the sour blanket and pulled off the buckskin dress. She couldn't be shed of them fast enough. Naked, she plowed into the dark waters of the nearby stream. Using sand to rub her body clean, Doe stood in the cold water and shivered. Hugging her arms to her body, she looked up at the pinpoint stars and wondered what she should do. Tell Sam what she'd overheard? Or let him think she'd come up empty?

An hour later, the sound of an approaching rider sent her scurrying for cover in the brush behind the Cottonwoods. The horse slowed as it neared the camp, a moving shadow darker than the night. When Sam, Colt in hand, edged into the circle of light made by the campfire, she sighed with relief.

"Sam!"

She sprang from behind the bushes, startling him. Spinning, he raised the revolver, then stopped as he caught sight of her.

Doe pushed the Colt aside and rushed into his arms. "You come back!"

"You scared the hell out of me, Doe." Smiling wryly, he shook his head, holstered his pistol, and wrapped her in a hug. "Of course I came back. And so did you, I see."

"Yes. I make coffee for you."

"Thanks. Let me take care of the horse and then we can talk."

Doe nodded and backed away toward the fire. Sam undid the cinch latigos and stripped the rig off the horse's back. Removing the bridle, the bit clanged metallic as he piled it on the saddle. Finally, he came to sit next to her by the fire.

"What do you know?"

He pouring himself some coffee. and shook his head. "Well, there's a helluva lot of drunks in Johnson Camp."

She took a deep breath. "Sam. Those men are here."

"What?"

"The men who kill your family. They are here. I see them."

"You're sure?" Sam bolted to his feet, spilling hot coffee on his hand. He cursed and dropped the cup entirely. "Dammit!"

"You burn yourself?"

"Never mind that. What did you see? Tell me!"

"I see three men in a alley. Hear them talk. They not see me. I hide." She pantomimed cowering behind the crates. "One called Digger. He see you at bar. He speak of you and is afraid you know them and what they did. Wants to leave. Second man not sure. Third man — they call him Cal. He mean man — tell them to shut up or he beat them."

"Digger? Cal? I've never even heard of them. Did you see their faces?"

Doe shook her head. "No, I hide, afraid they see me. But when it gets light, we find them."

"Dammit."

"Do not worry." She took his hand — the one he hadn't burned — and pulled him gently toward the bedrolls.

"I, uh . . . I doubt I can sleep."

"Tonight, we sleep together," she said quietly. Before he could protest, she silenced

48

him with a finger to his lips. Tonight would be their night. She needed him, and he needed her, too. She would prove to him she was a real woman and not a girl. And tomorrow, they would keep their promises to one another.

All of them.

Chapter No. 4

Sunrise came like a pin lampshade as they sat in silence eating her fresh bread and sipping coffee. The strain was obvious.

They each avoided talking. Dressed in her new outfit, she seemed like someone completely different as she hurried about packing saddlebags with food. Then she went back to kneel and check the coffee pot.

"Doe?"

She lifted her head and waited. Gently, he pulled her up from her chore and rocked her in his arms. Nothing needed to be said as they stood in the long shafts of light, close together. It was a while before he released her.

They rode into town. She sat the horse in her new outfit and held the reins. Sam went into the land office. He told the clerk he needed to find two men. One's first name was Digger and his partner Calvin. He also showed the man a silver dollar. The employee smiled and nodded that he understood he could earn it.

"I can find them." After going through some books, he came back and showed him a claim. Digger Sorenson and Calvin Denton had filed a claim on Red Horse Mountain. The clerk pocketed the coin and thanked him.

Sam looked at the map on the wall and saw the district the man had mentioned. The names meant nothing to him, but the perpetrators did not have to be familiar to him to have killed his family. He nodded his thanks to the clerk and headed back out the door. He swung lightly aboard his gray, took the reins from Doe, and turned the horse toward the western road out of the camp.

"You find where they are?" she asked.

"Yep. They've got a claim up on Red Horse Mountain. This road'll take us right up to the base of the peak."

Squinting under the shade of her new hat brim, she studied the country intently. A jackrabbit couldn't bob up in the low black sage that she did not see. The ruts they followed were a mixture of tracks — unshod mules, horses — one of them very large — and even a narrow buggy rim.

"Sam?"

He turned in the saddle. "Yep?"

"Will you know these men?"

"No. But thanks to you, it's the first lead I've had on them." He tossed his head and put spurs to the gray, setting out in a lope. Not to be left, her bay jumped in beside the gelding and kept pace.

The trail up Red Horse Mountain was barely more than a niche and a dry wash. Sam didn't mind the dry wash part. It was reasonably easy going and safe unless there was a sudden rainstorm on top of the mountain. The niche was a different matter. It appeared to have been a track followed by the elusive Dall sheep, or at best, some nimble mule deer. At places, their stirrups rubbed the bluff on the inside and hung over the ledge on the outside. Scrub pine clung to the rocky slopes. Emerging on top of a long ridge, signs of human activity and diggings could be seen scattered around under the sparse evergreens.

Riding up to a tattered sun-faded tent, Sam reined the horse up. "Hello, the camp."

"Hello yourself, stranger." A toothless, apron-wearing man in his sixties grinned at him from behind a repeating rifle.

Sam held up his hands, palms out. "We ain't highwaymen."

"I ain't stupid. I can see that's a mighty

52

pretty woman." The man grinned foolishly at Doe.

He clenched his teeth and tried to ignore the man's leer for the sake of the task at hand. "Where can I find Digger Sorenson?"

"You still got a three-hour ride. See them red bluffs?" The old codger pointed. "That's where you'll find that threesome."

"Three?"

"You deaf? There's Digger, Calvin, and big Donnie. Yeah, them boys sure have a good time. Come through here about sunup on their way back to camp. Told me they drank the town dry, loved every woman — 'scuse me, ma'am — and they was going to dig up a million in gold." The old man shook his head and laughed. "That Injun girl, she savvy English?"

"Not much, why?" Sam asked in a stage whisper.

"I'd give you a poke of gold fer her."

"I'll consider it," Sam said seriously, looking back at her with a sly wink.

Doe ignored them both. She studied the distant bluffs as Sam continued his talk with the prospector. The pine-cloaked ridge would not cover their intrusion. The fact that the three men they sought knew Sam when he didn't know them was a problem — especially if the killers saw them coming.

53

Sam bid the prospector *adios,* and spurred his horse up the path. She followed suit.

"I missed my chance to sell you back there." He laughed, reining the gray around a deadfall.

"It was not enough."

"Most he'd ever paid for a squaw."

"Yet you not take it."

"You're right." He reached over to pat her leg. "It wasn't enough."

She bit her lip and studied the distant bluffs at the top of the long ridge. "You think we may be riding into their arms?"

"Suppose you're right." He reined up. "What then?"

"We drop off on the south slope. Circle in." She made an around about sign with her free arm. "Take longer, but we might surprise them."

"Now you're thinking like a warrior."

A gunshot rang out in the distance, echoing across the ridges all around them before falling silent. They stopped to listen, but could hear nothing more besides the occasional grasshopper or small bird.

Continuing on, they heard no more shots, but picked up the growing smell of wood smoke the higher they rode.

Sam dismounted in a grassy meadow and loosened the cinch. The gray began pulling mouthfuls of the sun-cured grass through the metal bit.

Taking the canteen, he watched her unpack some bread that she had cooked before dawn from the saddlebags. Bringing the bread and jerky, she pointed across the far slopes south of them. A herd of black-tailed deer were picking their way up the slope. Too far to reach with a rifle, they moved undisturbed as they searched for tender food. Above the deer, the mountain rose in a great rock face to form the peaks above the timberline.

"Pretty country."

Doe shrugged and spread the food on a large rock. "One day I will take you to the land of my people."

"We'll do that." Sam bit into a biscuit.

Setting her Stetson down, she shook her hair loose and stretched her head back in the sun. Recalling the night before, she wondered if this night she would again enjoy him in their blankets. Perhaps, but perhaps not. The enemy was not far away. They had ridden in the warm mountain sun all afternoon until they were behind the bluffs. A faint trail of smoke wafted up to them from the diggings below.

She looked the little camp over. "You need the eye of an eagle for this."

"Something's wrong down there. There ain't any sign of a horse or mule. No one's working. They may know we're here and set up some kind of trap for us. You wait here, give me time to get down there."

She nodded and looked back to make sure the gray and the bay were tied up behind them. Checking Sunday's old pistol and shotgun, she watched Sam descend to the camp, sliding on his boot heels in the loose gravel. Pistol ready, he searched the first tattered tent from the rear. Empty, save for some trash and discarded bottles. Nothing but the wind whistling as his soles crushed the gravel.

He heard a moan. Whirling around, he found it came from a pit beyond. Waving for Doe to stay back, he cautiously approached the sound. Pointing the pistol out ahead of him, he found a crumpled form at the bottom of a hole in the rocky ground.

The wounded man looked up at him, both hands pressed against his bloody belly. He'd been gut shot.

"S— Sam Brennen?"

"Who the hell are you?"

"Digger Sorenson. I ain't got much time . . . figured sooner or later you'd show up. . . ." He coughed convulsively and clutched harder at his belly. "I didn't kill

56

your woman, Gawd is my witness. We was — crazy drunk that night. . . . And it was Donnie pushed the one girl too hard. The little blonde one. I seen her eyes every again ever time I — I close my eyes. . . . Cal . . . him and Donnie . . . they took the damn gold and shot me."

It took every bit of control Sam had not to grab the man up by his hair and beat him to death with his fists. "Why my wife?"

"I don't know where we was heading . . . aw, gawd, it burns like fire in me . . . if I could live it all over . . . get me a drink."

"I ain't got one. Who used the damn knife?"

Sorenson coughed again, only this time his eyes rolled back into his head and his body went limp.

Sam jumped down into the hole and grabbed him by his shirt front. "Tell me, gawdammit! Who used the knife on my wife and daughter. *Answer me!*"

Another cough, spattering blood all over the man's dirty beard. The eyes opened, but were now glassy, focused on something far beyond the grieving man before them. "It was . . . Cal . . . Cal. Watch out for . . . Tell ya he's plumb crazy. . . ."

Then he was gone.

Sam looked up. Doe stood above them on

the lip of the hole, the double-barrel leveled at the sprawled figure. He climbed out and pushed the barrel aside.

From the look on his face, she decided that the killer was dead.

"They are gone?"

"They rode out on the damn trail. Hell, they're four hours ahead of us,"

"They cannot run forever."

"You're probably right, Doe." Sam sighed, tired to the bone.

"We bury him here?"

"I guess so."

"Good, but we not waste another blanket. Dirt good enough for him." Handing him the shotgun, she turned and walked away, returning shortly with two rusty shovels. She peered over at the corpse as flies crawled over his open eyes. Without ceremony, she began pitching in the loose earth on him. Sam joined her without a word.

After a few minutes, he paused and looked to the blue sky.

"Lord take this soul into your trust and care. Amen."

"Short funeral." She shook her head and chuckled. "When *padre* does it, takes long time."

They went back to shoveling. Before long, they finally had enough dirt to protect the remains from all but the most determined creatures of carrion.

Sam threw down the shovel in one of the other shafts with a crash. He felt . . . empty. One of the men who had ended his life with Alicia was dead. The others were fleeing, getting beyond his vengeance. *Vengeance.* What vengeance? It was an empty curtain call. There was no reason to celebrate, no satisfaction to fill the void the loss of his wife and daughters had made in him. Damn their whiskey-soaked hearts.

He stretched his back and sighed. "We need to get back to the horses and get after 'em."

Wiping the beads of sweat off her forehead, Doe shook her head. "First, eat supper, then sleep. Break horses' necks going down that mountain in the dark."

"Suppose you're right."

She smiled softly up at him. "I am."

They brought the horses down from the bluff and set up their own camp. Once the fire was going, Sam dropped down on the ground beside it, exhausted.

"That man was nothing." He leaned back on his palms and studied the star-speckled sky. "I told myself, when I found those killers, I'd tear them limb from limb. Eat their black hearts raw! Instead, it's nothing . . . I feel *nothing.* Not mad, not sad . . . not a damn thing."

"You good man, Sam Brennen. Those bad men not worth dust on the wind." Kneeling, she hugged him tenderly to her breast.

"I just wish I knew what I was supposed to be doing."

She rocked him gently back and forth. "Right now? Sleep."

"Right now?" His hands slid down to her hips. "No sleep."

"We don't sleep much," she said with a grin.

"Who cares?"

"Good question." She rubbed her cheek gently against his bristled jaw. He squeezed her hard-muscled thighs.

Sam tried to picture the other women in his life he had known this personally. The pleasure he extracted from Doe was without restraint. Never had he experienced such an open relationship. The girl-woman had an innocent freedom about her that he had never known in his wife or any other woman.

By the time they were finished, the fire had died. Instead of rekindling it, they ate the last of their dry bread and jerky and rolled up together in the blankets for the night.

■ ■ ■ ■

Dawn was shaded by tall cumulus clouds, casting dark shadows on the ridge. Keeping a watchful eye on the bank, Sam saddled the horses. There was going to be a big change in the weather.

"May rain," she offered, swinging her skirt over the bay.

He shrugged. "We've got slickers. Let's get going."

Rain fell in sheets on the distant slopes, the sky split by lightning. They rode in silence, watching the storm sweep up the great wall of the Rockies, cool air brushing by them as they rode downward.

Adjusting his high-crowned hat against the gusty wind, Sam followed the hoofprints of their quarry until the deluge wiped them away. One of the horses had a broken shoe, and made a distinctive print with each step. That would make tracking them a little easier, at least.

Around midmorning, they approached "Toothless's Camp" again.

"How in the hell did yah miss 'em?" The old man was outside waiting this time, the rifle cradled in his arm like a fixture in spite of the rain.

"We went around the back way. Guess they told you they shot Digger?"

"That right?" He looked strained by the news.

"Yeah. Left him gut shot and took all the gold."

"Shot Digger, huh? Hell, they got awful edgy when I asked 'em if they'd seen that squaw man looking fer 'em. Cal sure did cuss a bunch. He really got mad."

"This Cal — what's he look like?"

"All whiskers. Got mean eyes. A big head like a grizzly and a big red scar over the right eye. That red scar goes clear around the top of his eye."

"And Donnie?"

"Big Swede, blond hair. That one ain't all there. Rock or two short of a load, know what I mean? But he's stronger'n any man I ever knowed. He don't know how powerful he is."

"They say where they was going?"

The old man shook his head. "Figure Big River Country. They've got a new strike up there."

"Thanks." Sam waved his head for Doe to follow.

"Hey! That offer's still good on her."

With a sly grin, Sam backed up alongside her horse. "How 'bout it?"

She smiled and shook her head.

"She'll get old, ugly, and fat. My gold won't!"

Sam laughed and turned away. "I'll pass."

Staring down into the old man's face as she passed, Doe sneered at him. "You old, ugly, and no teeth now! I got good man."

"I'll be gawdamn, she does speak English." The old man's eyes got wife and his voice rose even higher. "Hey! I'll double that offer!"

Sam chuckled to himself as the experienced horse picked his way down the steep trail. It was obvious to him, she had extracted her own vengeance on her would be buyer. She was no wilting flower, this one.

"I miss a lot of what you said to him?" he asked over his shoulder, amused.

She pinned him with a dark stare. "You better not sell this one."

"Why not?" He checked the gelding.

"You won't have any hot bread."

"Hmm, well as long as you don't burn it, I'll keep you." He laughed. Hell, he wouldn't take a thousand dollars for her.

The rain continued throughout the day and into the evening, pelting them with small hail by the time they reached their old campsite and set things up. She swished about in an oilskin poncho as the rain threatened her fire, drops spatting off the hot rocks with a continuous low hiss.

Doe checked the coffee and poured him a cup. A close crack of lightning nearly blinded them, and they ducked instinctively against the following crash of thunder.

"We're gonna need a tent if we're going to live out in this. Sleeping under a ground cloth and a slicker is never dry."

She squatted down beside him. "Need another horse to pack it, too."

"Yes, we would. Better see about that, huh?"

Impulsively, she kissed him on the cheek. "Good idea."

Cold air swept in after the rain, and long before dawn, they crawled out of their damp covers before they both caught the chill. Doe worked over the smoldering pile of damp wood and chips that had been their campfire in vain. Vexed at her own inability to get it to blaze, she spoke in angry, clipped Apache.

Sam stopped rolling up their bedroll. "What are you saying?"

"Stupid wood won't burn." She stomped her boot, casting a frown at him.

He peered over her shoulder. "It looks too wet to me."

"Hmm, you so smart, you build fire!"

He grinned. "Well, I guess I'll just have to beat you now."

Still angry, she threw a large chunk into the smoldering mass, and it blazed up. They both laughed at the incident.

"Where's Big River Country?" she asked as they finished eating.

"The probably went north. Denver, Cheyenne, maybe on up into Montana. All they know how to do besides kill people is mining. Lots of places there ain't no law in those gold strikes up there."

"One horse has bad shoe. Maybe they try to get it fixed."

"Maybe." So she'd noticed it, too. She was just full of surprises. He began loading their gear on the pack horses. How far ahead were they by now? Did he have time to send a letter off and collect that reward on Joe Sunday? What about to his friend — the judge up in Fort Collins — about Digger's last words so he could let the Denver police know about those two.

"You think Denver?" She frowned.

"More than likely. It's a big place, they can get lost there." He shrugged, saddling her bay as she put out the fire with a can of water. Even in a rain, a smoldering fire could start a prairie or woods fire.

Searching about to be sure she had not

left anything behind, Doe adjusted her flat-brimmed hat and mounted the brown horse. Sam gave a last test of the stiff ropes on the pack before handing her the leads.

Before the sun's first gray light, they were headed north through the sagebrush and bunchgrass along the foothills of the big range. Skirting Johnson Camp, they fell into the muddy wagon tracks on the main road. Sam kept checking the ground, but any sign of the men they chased had been washed away by the rain overnight.

Absently, Dhe checked her horse as he scuffed something metal with his shoe. Her eye was drawn to a freshly-thrown shoe in the red-brown earth.

"Here it is!" Doe reined up and bounced off the horse, keeping the first pack horse up close as she bent over.

"What?" He reined the gray back and turned around.

She plucked it out of the mud and held it up in triumph. "The shoe!"

By God, she was right! "Well, I'll be. . . ."

"They can't go far on such a horse?"

"Believe you're right." A new confidence filled him. They really were on the right track. Thrilled by the discovery, he dropped down and from the gray, picking her up and spinning them around in a circle until she squealed. "We'll track down these bastards yet, you'll see!"

"What is the next town?" she asked as he let her down.

"Gold Site. Over that next hill, I figure." He jerked his head back over his shoulder, off to the north.

She gathered up her reins to mount up and make the reluctant pack string follow. "Why you just stand there?"

"Yes, ma'am." He laughed, then vaulted back into the saddle. Notions floated through his mind about those blackguards. Had they caught a break? Were they finally getting close to them? He looked down at the broken horseshoe in his hand, then flung it off into the sagebrush.

They'd find out soon enough.

Chapter No. 5

They reined up in sight of the town. A scurrying crew of workers were tearing the buildings down as fast as they could move. They were loading tents onto wagons and ripping up the lumber floors. There must be another gold strike up in the mountains.

Gamblers, dance hall girls, and merchants were hauling down a big saloon tent as Sam rode up. A big man in a bowler appeared to be in charge, giving orders to everyone.

Sam rode over and reined up. "Mister, I'm looking for a man, got a large scar over his right eye and a big, blond Swede."

The superintendent nodded. "Rode through three, four hours ago. Wanted to know where they could catch a stage."

"Where's that?"

"Alkali Flats, about ten miles east. Rain may have slowed it down, but it usually comes through about sundown." The man held up a hand and stomped over to two men moving some glass windows. "Dammit, be careful! You dummies break those glass windows, and I'll pin your hides to a tree!"

"Yes, sir! Sorry, boss!"

The big man shook his head. Squatting down on the high porch, he turned his attention back to Sam. "What'd they do?"

"Robbed a man, shot him, and left him for dead."

"Hard cases, then." He shook his head and chewed on a plug of tobacco in his cheek. "They got a good start on you, I'm afraid, son."

Sam thanked him, reining the gray out and short loping over to where Doe held the pack string.

"They're making for the stage, about ten miles away. We got one chance to catch them before they get there. If I make a run for it, I may catch them. You bring the pack horses slow. I'll meet you there. No sense running all of these horses into the ground."

Doe started to protest, but stopped when she saw the look on his face. She simply nodded instead.

Already primed, the gray pranced around. Turning him, Sam let the long-legged steed have his head.

Watching them go, Doe jerked the bay and

pack horses into a hard trot. Using her heels, she kept the brown pony and the others in a trot, despite their reluctance. Bouncing occasionally in the stiff gait, she scolded her charges along.

The iron-colored gelding ran flat out on the soft road — ears pinned back, his long legs pumping ground as he reached for more with each stride. Nostrils flared to get maximum air to the great heart beating beneath Sam's girth. Sweat wet his shoulders and soon turned into foam. Breathing easier, the gelding seemed to get a second wind as he topped the sagebrush ridge, far beyond Doe and her charges. The land ahead was level as they raced on. Hooves drumming a rhythm, Sam kept urging the horse on.

With the wind in their face, they flew past a slow team of oxen and freight wagons. Waving, Sam leaned into the horse's gait, and they swept on. He could see the distant buildings ahead. He was sure he could make out the dust of a stage coming up from the south.

If the great horse's heart would last, they could intersect that line. He felt the steed weakening under him. Conscience would not let him push the gallant beast any harder. Unfolding before him, it was plain

70

how the stage would come and go before he could reach it. Sam considered reining the weakening gelding in, but there was still a chance. He topped the last ridge to see the vanishing boot of the coach pulling northward, fresh horses racing away from his vengeance.

Riding the heaving wet horse up to the stage stop, he hailed a green-visored agent. "Wait, mister."

"The stage has already left." The agent studied the snorting, foamed horse with his head low and sides pumping painfully. He pursed his lips in disapproval, then the agent looked up at Sam.

"Did two men get on that stage? One big and blond, the other with a scar over the right eye?"

"You run that horse that hard for them?"

"They're wanted for murder."

"They'll be in Denver, noon tomorrow." The man shook his head in disgust at the horse's condition.

Sam didn't have time for his disapproval. "When's the next stage south?"

A shrug. "Be one tomorrow, like today."

Sam dismounted heavily. "I need to get a letter on it to the Denver police."

Turning, he led the trembling gelding back and forth, up and down the dusty ruts.

He needed to walk him until he cooled off a bit. There was a sudden emptiness inside him that left him feeling weak. Had he pushed hard enough to catch up with the two outlaws?

Did he really want to?

Horses puffing and hooves thundering, Doe came sliding in hard under her flat-brimmed hat. Screaming "whoa" at her charges, she nearly collided with him in the last red light of day. Jolting in the stirrups to stop, she searched his face, then slumped in the saddle.

"Too late?"

"Yep."

Dismounting, she snatched the reins from him. "I will cool gray one."

"All of them need it. Why in hell did you race all the way here like that?"

"You need help. Come pretty quick." She ducked, then grinned at him.

"I'm sorry I yelled at you. We need to find a camp." Sam shook his head and hugged her shoulder.

She smiled in pleasure at the show of affection. "Dark now."

Sam tossed his head down the street toward a corral in the distance. "We can afford to put this crew up in the livery. God knows they deserve it after all this."

One by one, they got the horses soon cooled down and let them drink from a nearby water trough. When they reached the stables, the livery man inside hobbled over to join them with his yellow lamp. He kept stealing glances at Doe while they negotiated the price. Finally satisfied, Sam asked for some whiskey to rub down the gray's legs and led him into an empty stall to eat.

He nodded to the stableman. "Thanks for your help."

The old man sneaked one more look at Doe. "Fine, I'll check him a couple of times in the night."

"Do that."

Their horses munched grain noisily as he and Doe sat on the stable floor eating canned peaches and crackers in the dark. Their backs against the wall, they could hear a dancehall girl singing off-key somewhere down the street.

"I would rather hear a wolf howl."

Sam slurped syrup from his can. "Much rather."

"We go to Denver now?"

"No. I'm going to write a couple of letters. One to the Denver police. My friend, the judge in Fort Collins, will take a dying man's deposition. Then, I'll write Cheyenne for a claim on that reward for Joe Sunday."

"Take long?"

"A week, maybe. Are you in a hurry?"

"No." She laughed freely, leaning back against the rough boards.

Chirping crickets were busy with their nightly concert as Doe shut her eyes. This was a good time with a man she had never dreamed of. The warm sweet taste of peaches lingered in her mouth as she rested.

Answers came in less than a week, as it turned out. The judge's reply promised swift justice once the outlaws were apprehended. As for the reward for Joe Sunday, a bank transfer for fifty dollars from the Cheyenne-Laramie Lines came in on stage two days later.

The couple's new camp was set up on a thin, muddy stream. Cottonwood proved a poor firewood, though, and dry chips were at a premium. Doe had scoured the area in search of fuel and found nothing. She was ready for them to move on, and not shy about telling him about it.

"No damn thing burn here. Bugs bite all the time. Water is bad to drink. Why we stay here?"

"You mad?" He barely looking up from his repairs on the pack saddle. He'd heard this about a hundred times already.

"Nothing burns good here."

He nodded. "We'll head for the mountains tomorrow, okay? I'll have the horses all fresh shod, and they're rested and slick. Two days we'll be back in the mountains, I promise."

"Good! Why do white men live here?"

"Don't know. We'll head out early, okay?"

"Fine!"

Hiding a grin, he got up and stretched his back muscles. He was unsure of what they should do next. Give up the chase? Find a place to settle down? Those bastards who'd murdered his family were gone. With his descriptions in hand, maybe the Denver police would get lucky and find them.

Or maybe they wouldn't.

He glanced back toward the fire. The emptiness in his gut nagged at him. He owed it to Agnes and the girls to bring their killers to justice, didn't he? Yet looking at Doe as she fussed over her cooking, a part of him longed to simply put the whole thing behind him and get on with his life. A new life, with Doe, free from the pain and misery of the past.

The question was not whether he could do it or not. It was whether he could do it without looking over his shoulder for the rest of his life, wondering if or when those bastards would show up again to rob him of everything he loved.

CHAPTER No. 6

The time of an Indian woman's menstrual period is one of solitude and isolation. Doe knew before they reached the mountains her time was about to begin. She had hoped they would reach their destination before it happened, but luck was not with her there.

"Hey, get out some bread, would you?" Sam had stopped to let the horses take a break and was uncinching his gray. When no reply came, he glanced back over his shoulder. Doe had dropped the lead for the pack animals and was backing her horse away from the others, clearly upset. She looked like she was about to bolt. "Hey, what's wrong?"

"I go away! I am unclean."

"What are you talking about?"

She looked down at her knee-high moccasins, the tops of which were now stained red. "It is my time."

"Oh." Sam saw now what she meant. He

reached out and grabbed the bridle of her horse. "Doe, I'm not dumb about women. I was married for quite a while. My wife had the same thing."

"Not matter."

"You're right, it doesn't. This is a natural thing."

"Bad time to be near me."

"Calm down. We'll go ahead and make camp here. I'm not afraid of this."

"Apache men are."

Sam snorted. "I ain't no Apache, and we ain't got time for superstition."

"Then we must go on to the mountains. This is a bad camp." She sighed, relenting. Torn between two worlds, she believed that she must please this man. If he was a fool not to fear her unclean time, she must protect him in other ways.

He patted her leg to reassure her. "Soon as the horses get rested."

"When they are rested. Let us go on to the mountains."

They had made their new camp high the mountains by dark, at what she had come to call The Place of the Mockingbird. It was a good name for the site — a grove of white-barked aspen with a grassy bottom for the horses across a rushing, clear little stream.

Their new canvas tent, still so white it hurt her eyes under the sun, sat in the middle of the small clearing in the midst of the aspen grove. The western horizon was dominated by tall peaks, providing a gentle updraft to cool the warm afternoons. The steeper slopes were forested in pine, except for a few barren black rockslides.

Sam had ridden off at dawn to a place called Summerville for supplies and what information he could talk out of the locals, leaving her to tend to her morning chores. Saucy blue jays scolded her as she lifted the three-legged Dutch oven over hot ashes with her iron hook. Heaping red hot embers on the lid with a small shovel, she set the bread to baking. The horses were standing hipshot out in the meadow, swatting lazily at flies with their tails. Full of the rich bottom grass, they were content.

A mockingbird nesting nearby had dived at her several times already this day. Smiling, Doe feigned a wave and sent the brave split-tailed bird away again. Soft winds rushed through the aspen and played a song she knew as a little girl. Smiling to herself, she hummed along with it and began to move her feet. She was proud of the stiff new knee-high boots Sam had purchased for her in Alkali. Stiffer than deer hide, she had worked on them for hours, kneading them with gun oil to help soften the tops. Bending forward, she lifted her knees, testing the stiff soles. She could dance in them as she remembered in the camps of her own people.

Elbows close to her sides, she swung her arms up and down as she stomped in the Camp of the Mockingbird. It was good, but what dance was she doing? The Dance of the Eagles or the Victory Dance? It had been so long since she's been among her people, she couldn't remember. But it really didn't matter. She had not been so happy since she'd been pulled away from her tribe and her family so long ago.

A cold breeze suddenly chilled her bare arms. Doe shivered.

She stopped, peering about. It was not cold. Across the stream, the horses now stood stock still, their ears pointed.

Something was amiss.

Snatching up her pistol from beside the fire, she listened intently. Could it be a bear? Perhaps a cougar? Maybe —

A heart-stopping scream rent the morning air. Swooping in like eagles, four Indian braves on horseback appeared from the far side of the grove, and charged toward the camp. They were all young, thin, and bare-chested, their faces and breasts streaked with war paint. Feathers streamed from their long black hair as they rode toward her at full speed.

Doe didn't hesitate. She took aim with her pistol and pulled the trigger.

The Colt belched fire and smoke. One of the horses screamed and toppled over, rolling end over end and crushing its rider. A second shot struck a surprised lance bearer squarely in the chest. He flopped back off his pony like a puppet with its strings cut, falling to the ground in a cloud of loose arms and legs.

Veering off, the other two raiders headed for the stream and the horses beyond. Doe fired again and missed. She took a deep breath and steadied her aim. Her next shot caught the Indian on the left square in the back. He raised his arm skyward and pitched headlong into the stream. The last brave's pony swerved trying to avoid the body, then reared into a bucking fit. All the rider could do was hold on for dear life. The pony reared again, spun, and ran off toward the west with his tail tucked tightly between its legs, chased away by Doe's last two bullets.

Her hands shook as she poured black powder in the cylinders of the six-gun, then rammed a lead bullet in. She sealed each one with lard, so they did not crossfire. Her fingers still trembled as she put caps on each nipple.

Then she collapsed on her butt.

Both of the Indians on the ground just short of the camp were still. She still kept a watchful eye on them, lest they erupt. The one in the water hadn't moved, either. His pony, a thin paint with a feather tied in its mane, stood wide-eyed at the far bank. Blood had turned the little stream bright red.

Hoofbeats in the distance.

Damn! More horses were coming. Clutching the Colt tightly in her hand, Doe ran to the tent for the double-barrel, then took cover behind the packs nearby. If these were more Indians, she would be in trouble. They wouldn't make the mistake of rushing headlong into the camp like that a second time. Moving slowly, she raised the barrel of the scattergun and peered over the canvas packs . . .

She let out a breath she didn't realize she'd been holding.

All bluecoats and gold buttons, the cavalry troops splashed through the stream toward her, their little red and white flag fluttering in the breeze. A large man at the head of the column reined up just short of the camp and looked around.

"Sergeant, go see if anyone's hurt over in that camp." He leaned over to examine the fallen buck in the stream.

"Yes, sir." Spurring his horse, a man with yellow stripes on his sleeve spurred his mount up the sandy bank. Pulling up short, his eyes opened wide as Doe leveled both barrels of her shotgun at him.

"Whoa, mister — ma'am." The man, red and rawboned, swallowed hard. "Anyone hurt here?"

"Three, four Indians." She jerked the barrel of her shotgun at the ground.

"Sergeant Webster?" The impatient officer demanded. "What's wrong?"

"It's a woman, sir. And she's armed!"

"Good Lord." The officer rushed his horse across to join his non-com. Reining up short, he raised his hand. "We're friends. You speak English?"

"Yes." She dropped the barrel and turned it away. "I am called Doe. My man come soon."

"Thank you, ma'am." The officer turned and shared a look with the other soldier. Both men shrugged. "Ma'am, I'm Lieutenant Carlin, this is Sergeant Webster. We're with the B Troop, 6th Cavalry. We've been tracking these renegades for several days. May I ask, how . . . how did you manage to fight them off?"

Doe snorted. These men were not very bright. "Two guns."

The old sergeant cackled, then coughed to try to cover it up. His lieutenant shot him a warning glance. "You're saying you did this yourself?"

"Who else here?"

The officer blinked. "Well. . . ."

"Glad you come." She jerked her head toward the bodies on the ground. "You can bury them."

"Pardon me? I don't understand."

"Tired of burying no good outlaws! You soldier boys bury them!" Doe shook her head. Could this man not speak English? "Leave horses alone."

"Oh, yes, ma'am." The lieutenant dismounted. He gave his horse to an orderly, then turned at the sound of another horse coming toward them.

"Not worry. My man. Sam Brennen."

She grinned as Sam burst into view, waving a pistol with the wild look of a madman. Breathless, he saw the cavalry troopers, then leapt free of the lathered gray.

He looked around at the wreckage of the

camp. "What in tarnation has happened here?"

The lieutenant shrugged. "Your wife, I guess."

"You do all this?" With a furrowed brow, Sam searched Doe's face. She gave him a sly smile.

Answer enough.

All he could do was laugh. Holstering the pistol, he held out his hand to the young officer. "Sam Brennan."

"Lieutenant Alfred Watkins, B Company, 6th Cavalry." They shook hands. "We knew we were close behind these four renegades, but we were up on the mountain when we heard the shooting. Seems like the Mrs. here — ah, *Doe* — sent three of them to the happy hunting grounds by the time we got here. My troopers are rounding up the last one now."

The army officer turned as three troopers rode in with the fourth painted buck in ropes.

"Damn glad you boys showed up when you did."

"It's our pleasure, of course, sir." The lieutenant bowed. "If you don't mind my asking, though, sir . . . what kind of Indian is your wife?"

"Damned if I know." Sam pulled off his

85

hat and ran his fingers through his hair. "When she's angry, she starts cussin' in Apache, so I were a bettin' man, that's where I'd put my money. That's all I've got, though.

"Oh, no!" Doe screamed, then nearly bowled them both over scrambling toward the campfire.

"What, Doe?"

She looked up at him with blood in her eyes. "My damn bread burnt!"

The cold-eyed brave bound on his horse looked over them, ignoring the jesting guards as they pointed to the woman who had defeated him. His gaze never flickered when her angry eyes met his as she dumped the blackened bread on the ground.

A legend was born in the Camp of the Mockingbird. The Utes in the southern Rockies would speak of the "Many Guns Woman" who rides with the "Hunter of Men."

A burial detail buried the three dead Indians in shallow graves. Doe cooked more bread. Then, she baked more bread for the cheerful bluecoats in her camp. Watching her, she heard them whisper about the strange couple, but they were all polite and were delighted with her fresh bread.

After supper, Lieutenant Watkins offered

Sam a cigar. "If you don't mind my asking . . . What is your business, Mister Brennen?"

Sam cleared his throat. "Well, I mainly prospect these days. I used to be a lawman. Worked for Wyatt Earp in Dodge City for a while, then marshaled up in Fort Collins. I still collect a few bounties from time to time."

"I see."

"Lieutenant, while I was in Summerville, I visited with the Marshal there. He's an old trail buddy, and he tells me the Mulvain gang is up in this area. You haven't run across a Timothy Mulvain, have you?"

"Mulvain?"

"Yep."

The sergeant spoke up. "He means Potshot, Lieutenant. You know, up on Clear Creek."

"Oh, yes." Watkins nodded, now remembering. "Yes, we examined his camp earlier this year. We were looking for whiskey and any stolen horses with a U.S. brand. Couldn't find a thing. That's a dirty bunch, I tell you, though. Up to no good,"

They're wanted in New Mexico," Sam said by way of agreement.

The officer gave a sigh. "Unfortunately, we're limited as to what we can do in terms of civilian arrests. I saw nothing we could enforce. If you don't sell whiskey or guns to the Indians and don't steal U.S. property, then we have little jurisdiction."

Sam poked absently at the fire with a stick. "Is it an armed camp?"

The sergeant leaned forward. "Well, they didn't get ornery with us, you know, but we ride in with a whole company, Sam. Been different if there hadn't been so many guns, I'd think."

Sam chuckled "Probably."

"Excuse us, Sam." The Lieutenant got to his feet. "Your wife's bread has spoiled my troops, and it's getting late. We'll bivouac across the stream and head back to Camp Sherman in the morning. If you two ever need a job scouting, come look me up."

Standing stiffly, Sam nodded and shook his hand.

The officer mounted, saluted sharply, and moved off into the dark. The sergeant followed.

Doe slipped in beside her man as they rode off. Gently, she bumped her hip to his.

He dropped an affectionate arm on her shoulder. "Sorry I wasn't here."

"I was afraid it was bear. I am glad it was not."

He hugged her shoulder and shook his

head in disbelief.

"Aw, hell, girl. Four renegades sweep into camp, you send three of them into the ever after, and you're worried about a damned old *bear*?"

She did not dare look up. He did not understand. How could four men equal a bear? He has no fear in his heart for the bear.

My foolish man, I must watch him closely, for a bear has too much power even for him to overcome.

But what he did not know, there was no need to explain.

"I have a present for you," he declared as he unsaddled the gray and turned him free to join the others.

"What?"

"Here." He laughed and handing her a scarred brass spyglass.

Examining it gingerly, she frowned, perplexed at what it was.

Impatiently, he reached over and pulled it out to its full length and had her squint through the eyepiece. "It's called a spyglass."

"Spy — oh, I see! A speck is now big."

"We can see from a long way off now."

"Yes!" She was amazed by the power of the tube. Busy viewing everything on the mountain, the new gadget impressed her.

Once upon a time, she had viewed through such a thing at the mission but only for a moment — she became afraid that it would make her a red ant and be stepped on by a big horse.

"It will not make us small by its power?"

"Lord, no!" Sam chuckled. "Just gives you the eyes of an eagle."

CHAPTER NO. 7

Clear Creek was a larger tributary than the one they had camped on. Traveling light, they'd left the lead pack mare hobbled in order to keep the other horses close by. They studied the camp from a rocky slope with the sun high and behind them.

"Keep the glass down so it doesn't catch the sun," Sam warned, pointing at the spyglass. "We don't want them to know we're here."

Doe nodded, studying the pole corral in the trees. Saddles lay strewn about with a few Navajo saddle blankets thrown in, ostensibly for the five or six skinny ponies lazing in the grass. Three Mexican women worked around the cooking fire over a freshly killed deer. They looked to be busy making jerky and boiling some of the meat in a kettle. While the women worked, the four men all seemed to be relaxing in hammocks or sleeping in the shade. Brown whiskey bottles were strewn across the ground, and a few cur dogs stole an occasional piece of dropped intestine or bone.

"They look pretty sleepy to me." She closed the scope. Together, they turned and slipped back off the ridge toward the horses.

Sam shook his head. "Don't ever underestimate the enemy. Bad men like these live by their wits."

"So we just ride into their camp?"

"I think so. Put on your old buckskin dress and ride behind me like a squaw. Wrap the shotgun up in a blanket. We may get them to buy it."

She looked confused. "Buy . . . what?"

"Surprise them." He chuckled.

"I see." She carefully removed her ruffled blouse and skirt — she had just washed them. The old buckskins were in her saddlebags. They were not appealing to her anymore, but for the sake of the plan, she changed into them, anyway. She twisted her hair tight in braids and a string hat band. She carried "her baby" wrapped in a long enough blanket to hide the stock. Her face was dirty from the dust Sam had applied to cover her cleanliness.

Riding point, Sam cradled the Winchester in his arms, as one riding the mountains does.

The outlaws were still taking their *siesta* as they approached the camp. A cur dog started barking, waking a hulk of a man from his sagging hammock. He rose and stretched, chasing off his bare-legged female companion with a slap to the rump.

"Hello, the camp!" Sam hollered, riding forward.

"Hello yourself." The bare-chested man — who answered Mulvain's description — grunted, scratching his hairy chest. Sam caught sight of a gunbelt hung on a branch beside the hammock, noticed the man's hand hover near the holstered pistol there.

"This the trail to Bolgers Mountain?"

"Reckon you're lost, Squaw Man." The outlaw stretched his frame lazily. "This is a blind canyon, 'cept for a sheep-goat trail up the face of the mountain."

The others, awakening, looked up and examined the newcomers. If they were going to make their move, it had to be now.

Sam cocked the rifle.

"Make a move for that gun, Mulvain, you'll be eating daisy roots. Tell the others that Indian back there'll blow 'em plumb to hell!"

The outlaw leader must have had cotton in his ears, because he did exactly what Sam had warned him not to. The angry deafening report of the .44/40 made him draw back, shaking in fear. His hands held high, he searched about wildly for help.

"What the hell are you after?"

"That would be *you,* cowboy."

Waving the barrel of the shotgun, the hard-eyed Doe herded the other three men out of their hammocks and toward Mulvain.

"Get on your bellies," she ordered.

Reluctantly, they laid spread-eagled in the dirt, half-stealing stares back in disgust at their unlikely captors.

"It's hot out here," one protested.

Sam kept an eye on the women, making sure none of them made a move toward a hidden weapon. It was a good thing he did, too, as one — a skinny blonde girl — suddenly bolted for a rifle stuck behind a nearby barrel.

"Stop!" He aimed the rifle at her. "I don't want to hurt you, but if you force me, I've got no problem filling your belly with lead. You hear me?"

The girl sighed and raised her arms, seemingly defeated.

"Get out here where we can see you over there with the others."

With slow, sullen movements, she did as she was ordered.

Running out of patience, Doe grabbed her

by the arm and threw her in the dirt. "Find some ropes and sticks! You tie them up."

From his facedown position, the leader of the group looked over his shoulder at Sam. "Mister, we can pay you a lot of money to let us go."

"Not gonna happen."

Under the supervision of Doe and her shotgun, the blonde woman began trussing the prone men up. With a stick through the crook of their elbows, she bound each of their hands tightly behind their backs. Once they were bound, Doe pushed the girl away and checked her work. Twice she drew a long hunting knife from a boot and tossed it away.

Sam walked over to Mulvain and jerked the big man up, fashioning a noose around his neck. He did the same to the next man in line, a little Mexican man with dark, hate-filled eyes.

"Pretty tough, aren't you, *hombre*?" Sam looped the rope around the man's neck. "You must be the Mexican Kid."

"Te mataré a ti y a tu mujer, pinche pendejo."

He snorted at the insult. "Not where you're going, my friend."

Doe shoved the shotgun in the little man's back. "What he say?"

"Nothing worth translating. Don't worry

about it." He moved on to the next man, a skinny, freckle-faced youth. Sam hauled the kid to his feet, then paused to study his face. "Your name Mallory, by chance?"

"What's it to yah?"

"Nothing to me, but it's about seventy-five dollars in Santa Fe."

"You know what you can do with your seventy-five —"

He grinned and twisted the boy's arm, half-choking him into silence with the noose. "I think that's just about enough from you."

Leaving the kid gasping for breath, Sam came to the last man in line. He knew about this one, though they'd never met.

"Let me guess . . . you're the notorious Dress Ripper, right? You tore the dress off some Colonel's lady when you robbed that stage. Left her naked as Eve in front of all those folks." He looped the last noose over the man's head. "I believe the good Colonel will pay an extra hundred for your worthless hide. Shame them bluecoats didn't know about that, or you'd have been crow meat by now."

With the outlaws tied up and ready to be led down the mountain, Doe searched the camp for arms and valuables. Among other things, she found nine rifles, over two dozen pistols, and, oddly enough, a stash of expensive ladies' underwear. Once she'd gone through the tents, she started looking through saddlebags and paniers. It was really a sight to see. One after another, she dumped them on the ground, separating the spilled contents with a booted toe before moving on to the next one. Suddenly, she dropped to her knees to examine one item more closely.

Looked like she'd found something of interest. "Anything worthwhile?"

"Yes!" Her voice vibrated with excitement. Straining to pick it up, she hefted a fully-loaded money belt over her shoulder and brought it over to him. She gave him a triumphant smile.

Mulvain sighed. "Why don't you just take the damn money and leave us."

Sam laughed. "What money?"

"You think you're one tough sumbitch, don't ya?"

"Tough enough to sneak up on you, friend." With a jerk of his gun, Sam gestured for them to get moving. As they slowly filed past, Doe hung the heavy money belt on on his saddlehorn and went to mount her bay.

Sam cleared his throat. "Listen up! Your hides are worth as much to us dead as they are alive. If anyone tries to escape, you'll be facedown over your saddle. Got all that?"

They each nodded in turn, shuffling awkwardly after their former leader.

Taking one last hard look at the cowering women, still huddled together in the shadow of the trees, Doe wrinkled her nose. They disgusted her. Then it occurred to her that only a few short weeks before, she'd been just like them — dirty, dependent, afraid.

Then and there, she resolved never to allow herself to return to such a state. Never.

She turned to Sam. "Should I ride to camp and get our things?"

He considered this for a moment. "That's not a bad idea. Be careful, though."

With a raised eyebrow and the barest hint of a smile, she put heels to her pony and raced by the prisoners, spraying them with dirt and gravel.

"Hey!" Mulvain wiped his eyes as best he could with his hands bound together. "This ain't right. You aim to kill us? It'll take a week or more to walk to New Mexico."

Sam sighed. "Listen good, Mulvain. You'll live if no one tries anything. One wrong move, though, and I'll turn that Apache woman lose on you. You ever seen anyone fed to the ants?"

The Mexican Kid's eyes grew wide. *"Sí, señor."*

"Oh, shut up, Kid!" Mulvain turned back to Sam. "If you let us live through this, mister, I'll do some ant feeding myself when I find you again."

"I'm just as scared as I can be, Mulvain. Here, let me give you a little help to start your search. My name's Sam Brennen, and that woman with me is Doe. *If* you live, and *if* you ever get out — two very big ifs at this point — we'll have a warm reception for you when you stop by the homeplace for a visit."

"Brennen, huh? I'll remember that."

"Yeah? Good. Now shut up or you'll be walking barefoot to New Mexico."

The freckle-faced Dress Ripper gave Mulvain a nudge. "I think we all better listen, Boss."

Sam gestured with the pistol again. "That's good advice, boy. And you better start picking up the pace, too, or I may not let you live anyway."

Still grumbling, the prisoners began to clump their boots on the ground a little quicker. The gray worked up to a fast walk, and soon the outlaws were moaning to rest.

Sam ignored them for a time. If they were weary by nightfall, they'd be less of a problem to guard. Finally, he reined up and allowed them to walk as they half-stumbled out of breath.

The tall mountain range cast long shadows on them as they neared the main north-south route. When they came around the final bend in the side trail, he caught sight of Doe sitting astride her bay, waiting on them as though she didn't have a care in the world. She'd changed into her new outfit, and from under the wide brim of her hat, she gave him a knowing grin.

"The bad men walk pretty good."

He couldn't help but chuckle. "You clean up nice."

"Too much dirt playing squaw. Took short bath, plenty time to catch up with you."

"I sure guess so." He drew even with her and lowered his voice so only she could hear. "There's a boy with a wagon going to meet us about noon or so tomorrow so we can haul them the rest of the way in."

She gave him a questioning look. "You knew we would need wagon?"

"Figured on it." He nodded smugly. "Set it up in Summerville, but I figured it would take a day longer."

"How many days to jail?"

"We can be in Raton in three or four days. From there we'll press on to Santa Fe and let the law take them there."

"How much money?"

"More than a little." Sam reached over and touched her chin. "If we get there, why, we'll have more than enough to buy you a couple new blouses and new skirts."

As the sun started to sink behind the mountains, they found a high place on a ledge above the trail and made a dry camp without cover. One at a time, Sam released the outlaws and let them relieve themselves under his shotgun-enforced scrutiny.

He tossed Mulvain a length of rope. "Tie your feet up good."

"What kind of lawman are you, anyway?" the leader asked, looping the bonds around his ankles.

"Special kind of law, I reckon. Nearly starved to death keeping towns quiet, now I sleep outside, and all I got to worry about is getting your ugly hide to regular law."

"You and her really bounty men?"

"That's right, Mulvain, and you try one move, I'll dump your scalp on that Raton law's desk." Sam turned to the next outlaw in line. "Get on up here, Kid, you're next. And no funny business."

They gave each of the prisoners a cup of water, some cold bread, and hard jerky. While he took care of that, Doe built a small fire to make coffee and give them a little light to help them keep an eye on their charges in the dark.

After a while, Sam crossed his legs and leaned back against the rock face. "Why don't you get some sleep, Doe? I can wake you later on if I get tired."

Doe made a face and jerked her head toward the four tied-up men. "Who can sleep with all their complaining?"

Subtle as ever. She had a point, though. Mulvain, especially, hadn't stopped whining since they'd found him. By now, even his compatriots had to be sick of it.

"You know, Mulvaine, the bounty on you is worth just as much whether you're dead or alive. If you don't shut your trap, I'm going to untie your friends here and let them close it for you for a share of the reward."

Mulvain huffed. "My boys would never —"

The tired voice of the Dress Ripper cut him off. "I'd take some o' that."

Sam and Doe both laughed. In the light of the fire, Mulvain's face grew dark and his lips — closed now, for once — compressed into a thin, angry line. No matter how mad it made him, though, it had the desired effect and the whole crew finally lapsed into silence. After a while, they even all drifted off to sleep — or appeared to, at least. At Sam's side, so did Doe.

102

A few hours later, she stirred. The mountainside was pitch black around them. A thin quarter moon had set and even the coyotes had ceased to hunt.

"Did you hear that?" she asked.

"No." He shook his head. "What was it?"

"Horse nicker. Someone's close." She rose to a crouch, eyes searching the darkness. "Someone rides from their camp. One of the horses we took from them knows this horse out there."

"One of the women?"

"Perhaps." Those eyes of hers never stopped moving. "Wait here."

"Doe —"

But she was already moving. Six-gun in her hand, she stole off to the east in a low motion in the direction of the horses. Crouched, she moved in silence barely above the low sagebrush.

Sam listened closely even the night bugs had silenced their creaking. The only sound came from the horses grunting in their sleep.

He sat straight up as a woman's scream came out in the darkness, followed by Doe's harsh laugh.

"How many come with you, silly woman?"

"No one!" The woman's voice rose another octave. "I'm by myself. I came to help my man."

"Good place to die, stupid one. Get up there." In a few moments, two shadows appeared at the edge of the fire's light. The shorter one was Doe, prodding another, taller woman ahead of her.

Mulvain scurried to his feet. "Is that you, Rosa?"

"You better lay back down," Sam warned, cradling the shotgun. "This gun is kind of itchy."

Doe pushed the girl again, shoving her down with a force that sent her sprawling to the ground in front of the fire. "No gun, just one small knife. And she is noisy as a wild pig."

"Give her some credit, Doe. She managed to find us."

She laughed bitterly. "A blind woman could find the tracks we made."

"Break out some jerky and bread, we might as well get moving south." Sam readjusted his hat and sighed. "Listen up. I'm noosing you guys back together. No hands tied, but one bad move, and it will change my style."

"What about her?" Doe nudged to girl with one foot.

"Stick her on a horse and send her back north. She comes back, I'll let you use some of your Apache torture tricks on her 'til she's so ugly no man will want her."

Doe narrowed her eyes for an instant as though she didn't understand, then nodded. She booted the wide-eyed Rosa with her toe. "Get up! We go find your horse. Next time I chew you up."

"She'll . . . *what?*" The frightened woman looked at Sam.

"You better listen, *señorita,* and vamoose."

Doe led her away, gibbering about how she was sorry.

Mulvain cupped his hands around his mouth. "Rosa, come find me in Santa Fe!"

Sam chuckled. "She's a brave one, Mulvain, but I don't reckon she's *that* brave. Or that you're worth that much to her."

The next morning the road south was dusty and warm as their slow parade plodded along past a pair of freighters already moving north. Six slow oxen under a long whip slogged under the heavy load, urged on by tobacco-chewing teamsters.

Eyeing their odd little outfit, the wagon boss stopped his horse to visit.

"Keep 'em going," Sam told Doe as he reigned up. "I'll catch up."

The teamster boss spat tobacco in the dust between their horses. "Outlaws?"

Slumping in the saddle, Sam nodded. "Mulvain gang."

"You a lawman?"

"Bounty man."

"Figured so with that Injun gal along." The teamster grinned, taking plenty of time to watch as Doe brought the pack string past. "Not many hitched up with civilians got them a redskin housekeeper."

"Got a lot of freight on?" Sam ignored the man's lewd wink at the word "housekeeper."

"Army stuff only thing worth hauling these days. Those gold diggers are all fading on the slopes. Can't get a good load no-where." He spat again. "This one's going to Fort Sherman."

Sam shrugged. "Tell the Lieutenant there you saw us going south, would you? He'll know what it's all about."

"I'll do 'er."

"Thanks." Sam gave him a mock salute and loped off. When he caught up to Doe, she gave him a dark look from under the brim of her hat.

"White men never see a woman before?"

Past noon, Sam pulled up and pointed to a buckboard coming up from the south, the driver was trotting the team. When it got within earshot, the young driver sawed them to a stop.

"Mister Brennen, sir! are these them outlaws?" He looked down at the exhausted men that had just all collapsed beside the road.

"The very ones, Buck!" Sam grinned. "And this is Doe."

"Proud to know ya, ma'am." Buck lifted his hat.

Sam turned to the prisoners. "Okay, boys, get in the rig or get drug. One bad move, and you can run behind."

One by one, the weary outlaws climbed to their feet and got in.

Sam gave Buck the high-sign. "Let's go to New Mexico, Buck."

"Yes, sir!" The eager youth snapped, giving a frown at his passengers.

CHAPTER NO. 8

Raton was a busy place. Curious traffic followed them into the town. Teamsters with their wagons and burro train traffic had to be avoided. A crowd was following them from the boardwalk.

A bareheaded boy with a pencil and paper was half-running beside Sam's stirrup. "Is that the Mulvain gang?"

Sam nodded. "Same one. The whole gang."

"Wow! Say, could I ask you a few questions? See, I'm Mark Cowan, with the daily paper, and if I can sell this story, it would really help."

"Fire away, Mister Newspaperman," Sam said, reining in the gray behind the buckboard.

"Your name is?"

"Sam Brennen, and the lady back there is Doe Mockingbird." He indicated over his shoulder.

The youth peered back at her as she pulled through the traffic, a confused pack horse string behind her. Still half-running backwards, the reporter caught his balance on the buckboard tailgate.

"Can you spell all that?" Sam teased him.

"Yes, sir, but. . . ."

"Come around after I check these outlaws in. Who's the Marshal here?"

"That would be Marshal Kline. He's right up the street."

"That's where we're headed."

"How many shots were fired?" the determined newspaper man asked, unwilling to give up.

"One, near as I can recollect."

"One shot. Wow, and you captured the whole gang?"

"Saving ammunition. Now excuse me." Sam dismounted, visibly impatient with the questions.

"Yes, sir."

Tying the gray up, he walked around the hitch rail and shook hands with the Marshal. "Sam Brennen. Got a few boarders for your hotel."

Marshal Kline was a portly man with a smile under a fat mustache. He studied the Indian woman a moment and clapped Sam on the shoulder. "Strange bounty hunter,

Sam Brennen."

"How's that?"

"Ain't many bring them in alive. Most save the territory the cost of all but the funeral."

"You got any coffee?" Sam asked, ignoring the reference.

"Sure have. Come on in and rest your legs. We need to fill out some paperwork."

Pop! A blinding flash, and Sam ducked, jerking his Colt free in one cat-like move.

"Easy," the lawman cautioned. "That's just the photographer taking a tintype for the papers back East."

"Yeah." Sam holstering the gun. "I've been living by my wits too long."

Finishing with the business, Sam came out of the office and spoke to the youth standing by the buckboard. "Here's twenty dollars. Rest that team. Then get back home. You tell your dad you're a man. Tell him Sam Brennen said, a good one."

"Can't say I wasn't scared, but I appreciate it and getting to know you and her," he said proudly.

"Men say only fools ain't scared. Now, get that good team rested up and get home. They'll be expecting you." Untying the gray, he hailed Doe with a swing of his head as he pushed through the curious onlookers.

Searching, he found the telegraph office. Inside, he wrote a telegram to his friend the judge and the Denver police.

"What will I do with the reply?" the telegrapher asked.

"I'll be back and check, just hold on to it," Sam assured him.

"Yes, sir, Mister Brennen, we're doing lots of business since you brought in the Mulvain gang. I'm holding to send one out to New York City for Mister Clayton Whills."

"Good," Sam said, turning on his heels and almost bumping into a bespectacled man with a ruffled shirt and a pompous air.

"Clayton Whills with the *New York. . . .*"

"Sorry, but I promised a young man this story first," Sam said, touching his hat to excuse himself.

"How about a drink, old chap?"

"I'm not an old chap, and I'm not drinking. If you'll excuse me?" Sam was fast growing impatient.

"What is this local lad paying you?" the red-faced reporter demanded.

"I don't recall he said anything," Sam said, the irritation rising in his voice. "Well, that's settled."

"I'll double it, Mister — ah, Brennen."

"Get out of my damn way. You ain't getting no damn story from me." Sam frowned and pushed past him impatiently. Entirely upset, the puffed pigeon dude under the bowler stepped aside holding his paper and pencil back as Sam stomped outside. On the boardwalk, he searched about the wide-eyed crowd and shook his head slowly. "Where's the boy reporter?"

Then he saw him waving and coming through the crowd. He mounted the gray and booted the gelding to get them moving.

"Get up here behind me. I'm getting sick of all this crowd. Come on, Doe! We're going to find a camp somewhere."

Pushing the gray through the slowly parting crowd, he pulled the youth along behind. With a wave of his hand to her, they rode up the street. "Reckon they never saw a real Indian bounty hunter before?"

Under the brim of her hat, she barely grinned, more in the corners of her round eyes. "No."

They found a place at the foot of the mountain along a gurgling stream. Sam helped her unpack and tried to answer most of the youth's questions.

"Were you ever a lawman?"

"Worked with Wyatt Earp up in Wichita, then I worked around Fort Collins for a spell."

"This is going to make some kind of a

legend of the two of you," Mark said, shaking his head in disbelief.

"Golly, this may just be my big break."

"What outlaw are you going after next?"

"Ah, I can't say who that is, that would let them get ready for our arrival." Besides which, he had no idea himself.

"Oh, I never thought about warning them. Golly, I'm sorry. I wouldn't endanger you or Miss Mockingbird."

The newsman left them with his scribbled notes and refused the offer of a horse to return to town. Sam scratched his head holding the trail stained hat by his leg and beating it thoughtfully against it, he sighed.

"Who is Mockingbird?" she asked with a frown.

"Oh, I just thought that fit you. The white man expects everyone to have two names." Sam laughed. "Are you afraid of towns?"

"You saw them today, all crowding around looking like they never saw an Indian before. Hell, there are Indians all over that town."

"They do not wear nice clothes. They do not ride with a big man. They are not a woman, not a white man's woman."

"Who cares? What will we do? Did you not go to Denver because of me?" she asked softly.

"You've asked me questions I can't answer. Why did I not hate that man in the hole, he killed my wife . . . those little girls?" Sam sipped the coffee she brought him.

"What will become of us?"

"I don't want you to worry, we have money, we can go and ignore them."

"Where will we go?"

"The telegram first. Then we will catch a stage and go find the Peralta brothers."

"Oh," she cried and hugged his neck, sprawling him out on the sandy ground. Nuzzling his face with her cheek, she began to cry. He held her tightly as her wet tears soaked his face. He prayed for the strength he would need as he rocked her.

Sam rose with the dawn and rode with the busy quail that whistled to one another as they sought food. The streets of Raton were practically deserted as he rode slowly to the telegraph depot.

Dismounting heavily, he stepped inside. An older man worked the key intently tapping out the reply.

"Can I help you?" The man looked up.

"Sam Brennen. Is there a message for me?"

Searching through the messages, he finally studied one. He handed it across the counter "Yes, sir. Judge Walter Miller, Fort Collins, Colorado."

Sam Brennen c/o Raton, New Mexico Territory. X Man Donnie was shot by a house detective for assaulting a girl. X No report of Calvin Denton. Stop. At your service. X Honorable Judge Walter Miller. Fort Collins, Colorado.

"Hey, wait, there's one more," the clerk waved.

Sam stopped and turned back, then he took the paper. It was from the Denver police.

Donnie Sorenson shot by hotel detective assaulting woman occupant. X. Whereabouts of Calvin Denton unknown in this city.

He gathered up the reins and swung into the saddle without effort. Straightening up, he rode back up the main street until he reached the hotel. Dismounting out in front, he climbed the steps and crossed the worn, carpeted floor. Sitting down at a table, he waited for the waitress to take his order.

"Uh, I hate to tell you, but we ain't got a single egg in this house," she said, waiting and looking bored.

"Ham, fried potatoes." Sam took up the coffee she'd brought. With a swish, she left the table. He looked up as the Marshal strolled in, nodded, and came across to the table.

"Got room?"

"Plenty. Have a seat."

"Brennen, you're a strange bounty man." Kline shook his head. "Most men like you I know dump a bloody head out of a greasy sack on my porch. You rented a rig and hauled that mess up here."

Sam shrugged, considering this. He leaned back to survey the lawman. "That would have saved me some time doing that, and I'd have had to spend less time in the company of Mulvain and his likes. But I was law too long to pull something like that."

"Where's the Indian?"

"Out at our camp, she hates towns."

"None of my business. Thanks for settling part of my curiosity."

"How long before they send that reward?"

"It should be here in a day or two. If you're strapped for money, I can arrange a loan at the bank."

Sam shook his head. "No need, we'll make it just fine. But I do aim to head out for Arizona."

"Are you heading on down to Tombstone?"

Sam looked at him over the rim of his coffee mug, confused. "Why?"

"Old friend of yours is U.S. Deputy Marshal down there." The lawman waved the waitress over. "Steak, if it ain't tough, and plenty of beans." He turned back to Sam. "Mark said you used to work for Wyatt Earp. He's making plenty of headlines down there."

"Wyatt's a big boy. He don't need Sam Brennen."

"Why, all this publicity, you might get you a good job marshaling."

"Yeah, shoot a few mad dogs and settle a couple of domestic fights. Knock some drunks in the head, and end up getting fat or shot by a wild drunk."

"Well, it sure beats dying in some dry gulch with only some squaw to hold your hand."

Sam got up. " 'Preciate the advice."

"Hey, how about the meal?"

"I'll pay for it. I know where there's lots better food than this."

"You aren't that young, Brennen. The bounty trail will get yah killed."

"So will living." Sam laughed and tossed the clerk enough to cover the meal.

117

He was nearly mounted when the man in the Prince Albert suit came puffing down the street, waving his arms. "Brennen, wait, wait I say — God, man, this sniveling boy files a story about the greatest vigilante in our times and the damn wire service buys it. Now, if you'll trust me, I'll write a dime novel about you that will make us both richer than Titus Morehead."

"Who in the hell is Titus Morehead?"

"Why, the richest man I know . . . now listen —"

"No, *you* listen. I'm tired of talking. Go up to the jail and get your story from that riffraff. They can tell you plenty of lies about the wild west."

"Yes, they could. Well, sorry I bothered you if you don't want to be rich."

"Good." Sam reined the gray away.

He rode into their camp. Doe had pitched the tent, and he knew there was fresh bread. Pulling the bridle off the gray, he loosened him in an instant and let the saddle fall.

"Break out some peaches, I aim to get plumb drunk on that sweet juice."

"Drunk?" She leaned over to study his face.

"No, heavens, the last time I did that I sent Joe Sunday packing to hell and got me the best cook this side of heaven."

She shook her head and went searching through the panniers for the peaches. Finally, she raised a can high over her head with a whoop.

"Nothing like having an Apache on the warpath." He laughed to himself and shook his head. "What next?"

CHAPTER No. 9

They sold the horses and packs. That brought them close to five hundred dollars alone. In her new outfit — a very ruffled blue blouse, a long, full wool skirt, and a stiff-brimmed hat — Doe waited very conspicuously for the stage.

Sam wore a new brown suit and a white shirt with a string tie. The soft-brimmed hat was turned down in front, and the crown creased by skilled hands. All the way from Philadelphia, that hat had come from the best beaver, and the seller called it a "John B. Stetson."

In her rawhide boots under the new long skirt, Doe considered running away. All these white people made her uncomfortable, and someone wore perfume that burnt her nose. What did she think, it would attract a man like flowers? That man would hug a skunk who came after her smelling that bad.

120

Men were smoking cigars that smelled worse than bad fires in a rain. There was much to learn about being so close to white people. To eat with silver, not her fingers. *Do not eat,* was the answer to that, but she wouldn't make him mad. He was the best thing ever happened to her — Sam Brennen was like no man she had ever known.

He motioned for her to join him as the stage readied.

A very large-bosomed woman who smelt of that perfume was helped into the coach, another man next, then Sam helped her up with one hand. Searching, she sat in the middle, and Sam slid in beside her. Another man nodded politely and wedged on the far side.

"I certainly hope this trip is better than my last one, dear. It was so rough from Denver to here. Oh, my goodness, are you an Aborigine, my dear?" The woman across the stage peered over to look at Doe's hat-shaded face. The stage jolted out, and everyone inside bounced as the teams left the Raton station with a whoop and a holler.

"My name's Sam Brennen. This young lady is Doe Mockingbird, recent of Geronimo's Camp." It was only a joke.

"My God, you mean she's an Apache savage?" The woman fanned herself to keep

121

from fainting. "Tell the driver, my good man, that I want off this stage right this minute. I'll not pay good money to ride with, ah —"

"Hey! There is a lady down here wants out."

"Whoa," the driver screamed, and the coach slammed to a halt. Scrambling down from the top, the angry, canvas-coated little man jerked open the door.

"What in hell's name is wrong down here?" His face was turning red.

"I demand a refund. I shall not share this cabin with blood-thirsty Indians," the dowager protested, coming out of the coach like a ruffled hen.

"Well, you can stay the hell out and walk right back there 'cause I'll be gawdamned if I know what the hell you're talking about."

"Her!" She pointed a shaking, nervous finger at Doe.

"Lady, I've got a schedule, either get on or get out."

"I will report you to your supervisor!"

"Yes, ma'am, and tell him I need a raise. Throw down that damn heavy trunk, Tom," he said to the shotgun guard. The driver caught it and set it down unceremoniously in the dust beside the red-faced woman.

Climbing up without a look back, he left

the sputtering woman in the dust, mumbling about the things he put up with and gathered up his reins.

The stage rocked off towards Santa Fe. Sam decided that while stagecoaches were much faster than riding horses, they were also very bone jarring. He had forgotten that Santa Fe was a big place with narrow adobe canyons for streets. The hotel where they stayed was cool and seemed to shut out the world of shouting vendors and bustling people. The room had the rugs of the Navajo on the tile floors. There was more to this world than she could even think about.

"I ordered food sent up so we could eat here," Sam said, lounging on the bed. "You ever been to Prescott?"

"Prescott? What place is that?"

"It's in Arizona, and Joe Sunday had a good claim near there before his past scared him into running off."

She shook her head. "Too much going on for a dumb woman."

"Listen, get tough, girl. Anyone that can capture outlaws can whip civilization. You can show them!"

"Sometimes I think I'm losing."

Sam laughed and shook his head. Then someone knocked.

123

"That's our food. Open up the door, and we'll see what they've got for us to eat."

Doe staggered under the weight of the tray the man handed her.

Sam jumped off the bed and steadied her. "Man, we have plenty of food."

She set it on the small table. "Crazy white man about knock you over with his food."

He hugged her shoulder. "That wasn't how he should have done that."

She hugged him. "I have you. I can do whatever you need me to do."

"I know. I know."

The Santa Fe train station was a busy place. There were several men standing on the platform — men in buckets for hats and puffy pants with tall, shiny boots. Some had soft little wool caps that looked like a tortilla with a brim. Women with little sticks that made shade and ruffled dresses and big rumps that waggled after them.

Sam stood beside her as the train roared into the station, breathing fire and blowing dirty smoke and cinders all over them.

The whistle almost deafened her. Climbing the steps, she looked to him, and he nodded as she chose a set of seats, sitting down on her skirt as she smoothed it like she had seen the women do and swinging her boots under the skirt above the car floor, convinced that she had pulled this one off.

She watched as the train pulled out with a jolt not to equal the stage, and a man came by punching tickets. He wore a special hat and acted like he was in charge of the rocking train as it roared faster than any horse could run. She watched the flying countryside as the train moved westward. Doe pointed to some deer that bounded off across the juniper country.

The Harvey House served them great food in Gallup, and the train was off again.

The night swept them across the painted desert, and the cool, piney air of Flagstaff filled her nose. In the early morning light, they descended on the steady wooden boards of the platform. Sam carried the small case and guided her along in front of him. Their trunk would be unloaded and kept for them at the depot.

"Hey, mister, need a lift?" a buggy driver asked.

"Where do I find a livery stable?" Sam inquired.

"Give you a ride there for two bits."

"You're on. Get in," Sam said as he boosted her in.

Pine clad, the steep slopes rose above the

bustling railhead. The giant San Francisco Peak, like a great lump of rock, dwarfed the busy lumber town. Big logs on giant wheeled wagons being hauled by oxen lumbered up the streets.

The livery stable was built from bark slab, and the man who ran it was a burly lumberjack in an Indian blanket coat. "Our friend here said you are the horse man." Sam extended his hand.

"John Swain."

"Sam Brennen," he said, searching the pens.

"Got all kinds, in fact, I've got a great Kentucky horse that can out-run any horse I've ever owned. Then I got some good stout mountain horses that can stand up on the steepest trail. Whatever suits you."

"Mountain horses sound better to me," Sam studied the lot.

"Any here suit your fancy?" The big man turned back to inspect the woman standing behind them with her arms folded in her bright blanket coat.

"The copper colored lineback looks a little small?"

"Tough kind, that mare could carry you to Tucson and back."

"Catch that buckskin, too," Sam said, still studying the herd. Interrupted, he heard a mule bray and saw that Doe was studying one in a board stall.

The horse trader acted put out. "Tell that Injun that mule ain't for sale. I'm sending him to General Crook."

"She don't understand English," Sam said softly and pointed out a stout, bald faced, stocking-legged sorrel.

Swain soon had the horses sorted out, looking back in disgust as she fed the mule handfuls of hay.

"This blaze-faced sorrel is five," he said as Sam inspected his denture. "The lineback you chose is about four." Swain opened her mouth for Sam to see.

Satisfied, Sam nodded. Then he walked over to take a look at the object of Doe's fascination.

"Mister, that mule is worth one hundred bucks down in Fort Grant," Swain said, acting nervously perturbed.

"Make it seventy-five up here."

"And not a damn cent cheaper."

"You have a deal." He turned and hollered at her. "Doe, that's your mule!"

She never turned or nodded, simply bent down and fed it more hay from her hand.

"She hear you?"

"Who knows? Give you a hundred for the three crow baits."

"You want to buy my best horse for nothing," Swain protested.

Sam grinned. "He never cost you much."

"Lord, yes! Why that sorrel cost more than you're offering for all three," the livery man countered.

"You got cheated. He's got two splints on his front legs."

"They ain't hurting him."

"Not standing in this pen."

"The mule — which I'm losing money on — and the horses for two hundred fifty total. Take it or leave it."

"Give you two twenty-five, and you're cheating me." Sam shook his head. "But, I ain't got all day to dicker with you."

"You're a hard man to deal with." Swain moaned. "I'll take you up on it, and I've got a Texas made saddle that is a real bargain?"

"Tree broke in it?"

"Come on, you traded me out of the best horses I've got," Swain said, heading for the clapboard office.

Sam bought the saddle and a smaller worn but sturdy Army saddle for her. Picking out two pack saddles and some halters and two bridles, they argued over some saddle blankets and the whole outfit came to three hundred fifty dollars.

"Mister Brennen, wherever you learned

about horses and trading, they sure must have give you a good lesson." Fascinated by Doe, Swain watched hard as the girl saddled the silky-coated mule and tied it up, then began to help Sam with the others. Obviously perplexed, he leaned against the corral fence. "What business you two do?"

"Oh, we've got a claim on a gold mine a fellow left us in his will." Sam smoothed out the blanket and hoisted the pack saddle on the sorrel.

Swain wrinkled his nose. "You ain't going to ride him?"

"Right now, that little tough line-back mare's got a better walk to keep up with General Crook's mule."

"Suit yourself." The dealer shook his head in disbelief.

"Ready?" Sam turned to her when they finished saddling horses.

"If General Crook's mule is." She grinned and swung aboard.

Swain gave Sam a frown. "I thought she couldn't speak English?"

"I said she did not understand English — mostly no!"

"Hey, Sam Brennen. . . . Now I think of it, aren't you the one in the New York newspaper I read about?"

"Never been there." Sam smiled, and with

a wave, they left the yard.

"Hey, you're the big bounty hunter they talked about. I read the whole thing! That's Doe Morningbird. I'll be damned."

"Mocking*bird*," Sam corrected him.

The livery man took off his hat and scratched his head as they rode back towards the depot.

Sam checked out the trunk from the agent and began filling the panniers with their cooking gear. The tent was put on top, and she took out the double-barrel, cocked and loaded it with a click, then stuffed the Colt in her saddlebags.

In a short while, they were paralleling the tracks headed for the mercantile. Sitting on her mule waiting for him to come out, Doe felt less conspicuous because of the number of Navajos who were milling about. They spoke nearly a common language with her own people. It was good to hear words that she knew like white men in different towns could understand each other. She knew these words.

Two young Navajos were discussing her, thinking she could not understand.

"This woman is with a white man who is inside buying things," one said.

"Does she belong to him?" the quiet one asked.

130

"Yes. A foolish white man who wastes his money on such a good mule for such an ugly woman."

"You are jealous of the mule and his woman."

"I could take this woman from this white man if I wanted her. No need, but if I wanted to, I could." The boastful boy wrapped the blanket around himself tighter.

"I don't think so," his friend said.

"You are very impolite," Doe said in their tongue. "I would not leave this man for a hundred boys like you — or this mule, even if I had to walk after him for a mile."

The crowd of many-skirted women tittered in laughter, then looked away in embarrassment. Pleased, they continued to chuckle as Sam returned with his arms full. Searching about, he could see something had happened and saw a very embarrassed young man with his head down, leaving the informal gathering. He did not understand the chiding that the boastful one was taking from his companion.

"At least you didn't shoot 'em," he said very softly as he passed her stirrup.

She acted as if she hadn't heard him.

With him gone back inside after more of the things he'd purchased, an older woman with a turquoise silver necklace around her neck stepped out of the huddle. She asked Doe, "Are you *Diné*?"

Doe shook her head. "I am not of your people."

"Then you are Apache. I thought you were by your speech."

"I was once. As a girl. Now they call me Doe Mockingbird."

"I am Mary John. You have clothes like a rich, white woman."

"He has bought them for me."

The woman nodded, and continued on in Navajo. "Could I ask? Are white women nice to you?"

"I do not know. Some are afraid, others think I am dumb and cannot read or write."

"You went to school?"

"Yes."

"It is good to meet you, Doe Mockingbird." Mary bowed and took a step back. "Thank you for talking with me."

Doe nodded back, politely. "Yes."

Sam carried out the last load of items, including a stack of canned peaches.

Doe spoke softly to him. "Give the one with the silver-green necklace a can from me."

"Sure," he said, putting the goods down and walking over to the surprised woman to hand her one.

"From her." He pointed at Doe.

The genuine smile of pleasure spread across her brown face, and in English she said, "Thank you."

CHAPTER NO. 10

Riding south on the Lake Mary Road, Sam reined the small burnt orange mare in beside the mule.

"Do you like the silver the Navajos wear?"

Doe nodded. "They have some nice things."

"It isn't bad to wear their jewelry?"

"No, but I do not have any." She looked puzzled.

Reaching in the pocket of the Mackinaw, he swung the silver turquoise necklace he had purchased for her on his hand.

"Oh! It is very pretty."

"Good. Since we sold horses and bought mules and all, we still had enough money for it. Thank Joe Sunday."

"Maybe him worth old blanket." She giggled as she put the jewelry around her neck with her hat in her lap.

Sam was in no big hurry. They allowed the horses time to stretch their stable muscles. It took them three days to get to Camp Verde, dropping out of the high country of pine down into the warmer juniper-pinyon and the red rock country below the Mogollon Rim.

Passing two mule-teamed army supply wagons struggling up the steep grade out of the valley, the cursing non-coms slapping the reins turned to stare at the twosome.

"Hey, squaw man, she may scalp you in your sleep."

His cohort slapped him. "Stupid."

"That's a Navajo, see that silver necklace?"

Sam and Doe ignored the hoots and catcalls and rode the dusty narrow road that clung to the mountainside past the wagons.

Sam chuckled as he rode beside her. "Now you're a Navajo."

"At least I did not shoot them." She booted General Crook into a faster walk and jerked the lead on the reluctant pack horses.

Camp Verde was a dusty log and tent army outpost surrounded by the small green patch farms that watered out of the Verde River as it wound its way southeast. The town was made of clapboard buildings, and Sam stopped at an office marked Marshal. Dismounting, he tied the mare at the hitch rail as a tall, stern looking, silver-badged

135

man looked down his nose at Sam.

"Sam Brennen, Fort Collins, I was wondering if you could tell me how far it is to Prescott?"

The lawman eyed him coldly. "Sam Brennen, that Injun your wife?"

Sam grew aggravated at the man's attitude. "Excuse me?"

"There's a law in this territory that any man marrying an Injun, black, or Chinese is guilty of a felony."

"Glad she's not my wife, then. She just takes care of my horses. The road to Prescott?"

"That way." He pointed nearly due west.

Sam undid the reins slowly. "Wonder if you ever heard of the Peralta brothers, maybe?"

The lawman shook his head. "They don't live around here."

"Guess not." Sam swung aboard the mare. "Nice to meet'cha, Marshal." He touched his hat as they rode out.

"Yeah, I better not find out that's your wife, Brennen. This ain't Colorado, and we don't take kindly to white men marrying damn savages!"

"I appreciate the advice." Sam turned to ride off.

They rode in silence up the street, dodging buckboards and pedestrians who turned to study the strange twosome with the pack train.

After a short stretch across the valley floor, the road they followed took them up a steep winding grade for several miles. Taking it easy on their horses, they camped on a narrow bench with a spring about four miles north of Mingus Mountain. After they dumped the saddles and packs, Sam hobbled the horses so they could forage among the rocks and scrub without wandering too far.

By the time he was done, Doe had some bread baking and was boiling beans and coffee. They both kept close to the fire when the sun went down. With few trees to break the wind, it was plenty cold up there near five thousand feet.

Later, finishing their beans, she looked across the plate at him. "Pretty lucky you did not shoot off the shotgun back there?"

Sam shook his head, amused. "That guy was sure friendly, wasn't he?"

" 'She takes care of the horses.' " She mimicked his deep voice.

He set down his tin plate and fell over laughing. "One thing for sure, we have lots to learn about Arizona."

The next day was spent with more climbing the switch-back trail passing through gardens of rough red or yellow boulders bigger than any house they'd ever seen, interspersed with dense pine forests. They rode all day with only brief stops to rest the horses or water at a stream. Doe seemed delighted with the small herds of deer and antelope, flocks of wild turkeys and even a solitary buffalo cow along their trail. High on top of the mountain, Sam reined off to make a dry camp in the pinions. This time, there was plenty of grass for the horses and mule, so he put them on picket pins to allow them to graze.

Prescott was beginning to show the permanence of brick and brick paved streets in the clear pine-scented mountain air. The palace-like courthouse in the square was faced on the west side by a block of fine saloons called Whiskey Row. Sam left her with the horses and climbed the stairs to the scarred wooden-floor of the lobby.

The land office was quiet as he stepped inside. He saw a bespectacled man under a visor. "Perhaps you could help me?"

"Got a claim or homestead?"

"This friend of mine filed this up here two years ago and sold it to me in Colorado. Kind of wonder if it's of any value?"

"Hmm, just a claim? You got an assay

report?"

"Just happen to have one."

"Looks good enough, but it would take more than just this to sell it if that's your intention. You would need an engineer's report and examination. Do you want to sell it?"

"What's it worth?"

"Could be worth, oh, maybe a thousand for a quitclaim. It's in a good area, I don't mind telling you."

"Who buys them?"

"A man named Alex Thompson." The clerk looked at the clock. "You can find him across the street at the Palace Saloon about now."

Sam thanked the man who stole a last mute look at the claim and shuffled back to his ledgers.

Stopping to tell Doe where he was going, he crossed to the two-story saloon and entered its sour whiskey, beer, and smoke smelling interior. It was practically empty except for a few at the long, polished bar and a couple of bar girls busy talking in a booth.

"Alex Thompson?"

The bartender nodded to the sharp dresser at the middle of the bar. Sam thanked him and walked over to the man who seemed entranced with his own reflection in the mirror on the back bar.

"Mister Thompson?"

"Indeed, at your service, my good man."

"Sam Brennen. It seems the cards have dealt me a claim here in Yavapai County, and they tell me you're the highest bidder over at the courthouse."

"Have a beer?"

Sam nodded. Thomson waved with a two-finger signal to a ready bartender and two mugs of amber ale appeared in front of them.

"Now, let me see the claim." He pulled a monocle from his pocket to view the paper.

Sam followed it with the assay report as he leaned on the bar and studied Thompson. This man was no fool. Like a good card player, he never showed any emotions as he read the papers.

Finally, he looked up and brushed his mustache with a finger.

"Certain investors might buy this, but it would be required to have some more engineering reports — and of course time, which you do not have."

"I'm heading south. No rush. I'll wire you, and you can let me know." Sam folded the papers up to take with him.

Finishing using a short pencil to take

down the information that he wanted, Thompson looked at himself in the mirror again as he slid the paper inside his coat pocket.

"It could be a very good claim — understand, I only handle the sale on a commission basis."

Sam nodded "My pleasure, I'll wire you in a few weeks."

"Wait, I have another beer coming —"

"Oh, sorry. I don't drink anymore."

"That will be fine, Mister Brennen. It has been a pleasure to talk business with you. I shall see what we can do." The two men parted company.

Taking the reins, he searched about, but there was no gathering to greet him. He swung into the saddle, and they rode south out of Prescott. Dropping lower, they soon left the evergreens of pinyon and juniper for the cactus and warmer desert lands. Spiny ocotillo clung to the gravel hills, and soon the giant saguaro towered above them as they rode under the hot, fall sun.

Three days later they were in the oasis of Phoenix. Smokey gray mesquite trees lined the ditches that carried the murky water to the green fields of cotton, melons and corn. Sam had never seen the red pomegranates that she peeled as they rode through the valley, enjoying the seeds of the tangy fruit. He decided, if there had been a Garden of Eden, certainly they were riding through it. Indians drove skinny horses to wagons — their women whipped the team into a stiff trot. Wagons of sweet hay were hauled with horses and farm boys, and boxes of fresh produce were carried by wagons and teams on the way to market. Milk cows grazed in succulent meadows, some flooded with irrigation water, and killdeer chased the bugs trying to escape the liquid. Cotton grew taller than a man.

Sam stopped in the Phoenix Marshal's Office, and after a short conversation, returned with two papers in hand. Standing beside her stirrups, he handed her the posters. Slowly, she considered the crude facial drawings, reading the words with her lips and nodded.

"That the Peralta brothers?"

Sam swung into the saddle. "Yes, both of them. They call one *Bigote* because he has a mustache. That's the one the paper calls Jesus Navarro. The other is José Guillermo."

"Looks to me like they're wanted for several crimes."

"That's an understatment." He guided the mare east through the traffic of wagons, carts, horseback riders, and even some bicycles on the brick streets. Most folks on Washington Street ignored them except for a curious few who gawked from the horse-drawn streetcar as it headed into the city.

The wagon yard looked like the place for them to stay, Sam decided. Turning in, he dismounted and met the anxious youngster who ran out to greet them.

"*Señor,* to feed this many horses grain and hay is fifty cents. To build a fire will cost you ten cents for firewood, and there is no charge to sleep. Okay?"

"Good." Sam wearily dug out the coins to pay him.

"*Gracias.* I will bring you the wood right back." He rushed off.

Doe dismounted and stretched her back. Sam moved past a wagon and began tying the horses to the board fence. The chore of unsaddling barely was started when the boy returned with a big load of firewood sticks. The youth dumped them unceremoniously near the fire ring.

The boy accompanied Sam as he brought a generous fork of alfalfa for two horses and went after another. He pointed. "That mule sure looks like General Crook's mule that I saw one-time last spring."

"That's his name." Sam laughed as he set

the panniers down in a small circle behind Doe who was breaking the wood up to build a fire. With a sulfur match, she lit the fire that began to take hold.

Taking the broken white corn brought in a bucket for horse feed, he put it in the feed sacks and put them on the horses and mule. Kept them from fighting so bad for his two cents.

Outhouses were probably the worst thing Doe could expect. In the Santa Fe Hotel, the room had a pot she traded for an empty one. The wagon yard had a facility that was built from used rough lumber. It rattled dangerously when you slammed the door. Barely what she considered privacy, Doe found it too smelly to stay very long. She decided that demons surely were in such a bad place and kept aware the entire time spent there.

During their supper, a *vaquero* came by, doffing his large sombrero politely, and stood waiting to talk to them. Sam looked up in the last half hour of red light at the gray-bearded stranger.

"*Señor?*"

Sam rose to his feet. "Hello, my friend."

"*Gracias,* sir. I am on my way back to the *ranchero* and find I have little more money to feed my patron's horse."

144

"Sit. We have plenty of food. It is poor in quality but lots of it." Sam showed him a place to sit. "We can feed him some grain after we eat."

Doe stayed him with a hand and dug out a plate and spoon, dipped up some beans and handed them across the small fire.

"Muchas gracias, Señora." The man nodded politely.

"Sit with us." Sam motioned, and she poured him a cup of coffee. After he sat down, she handed it to him.

"I am embarrassed that I am so poor, but my daughter is going to school here and will be a teacher. It takes most of my wages to keep her here."

Sam ate slowly and studied the old man over his fork. "What ranch do you work on?"

"I work for *Señor* Mendoza. He owns a ranch on the Iron Mountain, and his cows run in the Superstitions."

"Is it a nice ranch?"

"I think so. But, the *Señor* lives in Globe because the Apaches sometimes camp on the land. He and his family have not lived on the *ranchero* since his father died. I watch his cows and brand them and drive out the big steers."

"Does it have a nice ranch house?"

"It was a grand place when *Señor* Mendoza's father lived there. The ranch house is big like the one on the hacienda where I was born in Chihuahua."

Joining their conversation, Doe said softly, "The house was once white, and the tile was very red."

"You have been there, *Señora*?" The man sounded excited.

"Yes."

"Did you visit the Mendozas?" Sam asked.

"No, I was a little girl then and remember you."

"I do not know you. I am sorry."

Sam dipped out some more beans. "Tell him, Doe, who you were with."

Doe gave him a questioning look. "Does he have a good heart?"

"I am sure this *vaquero* is a very strong man." Sam chuckled.

The man stopped eating his beans and looked closely at her.

She cleared her throat. "Do you remember when Natise came and spoke to the old man Mendoza?"

"Oh!" He swallowed hard and nodded with big eyes.

"Natise and the older man sat on the tile porch and spoke for a long time."

"Yes, the Apaches had an agreement with

146

him for years. They could eat a calf when they were without food."

"Why does the young patron not live on the *ranchero*?" Sam asked.

"He does not think it is safe. There are still some renegade Apaches. His *Señora* does not like the isolation."

"Would your patron sell the *Hacienda*?"

"I do not know, but you may go to Globe and see him."

"How many cows?"

"I think you could find perhaps seventy-five."

"*Corientes*? Longhorns?"

"*Sí, Señor.*"

"Should we go see his patron about this place?"

"You will like those wild mountains?" He could see the excitement growing in her brown eyes.

"Would you stay and help us?"

"*Señor,* my name is Miguel Santos, and I would be proud to be your *vaquero.*" The man's dark eyes glistened with excitement at the prospect. The three talked on about the ranch and the country. One thing Sam understood well — both this *vaquero* and Doe liked the area up there.

Later, Miguel excused himself after thanking them for the meal and horse feed. Sam invited him to breakfast and to ride east with them. He said he would and left.

"What do you think of such a place?" Sam stretched his arms and yawned. It had been a long day.

"It is a very nice place, but there is no wagon road to that place. Not when I knew it."

"You go in on horses?"

"Yes. No road. Do you think he will sell us this place?"

"We shall see." Seated on the ground, he cupped his hands behind his head and grinned as she finished washing the dishes and pots in steaming water.

"Some things are too good to come true. I can remember the shiny red tiles on the floor. What if we do not have enough money?"

"That's for me to worry about."

"I will speak to my gods and the one the Padre loved." She tried to suppress her obvious anxiety.

"Do that, Doe." He liked the notion of a remote ranch, especially one where she acted like she would be happy to live. She had become someone important in his daily life.

CHAPTER No. 11

After breakfast, the three of them rode east through the clean, wide streets of the Mormon town of Mesa. The great wall of the Superstitions rose to the east in its purple blue majesty.

Sam could sense by the way she squinted to see the mountain's face that Doe was anxious. The mule, he decided, felt her nervousness, too, through the harsh pulling on the bit and sharp heeling in the ribs.

"*Señora,* have you been to the place where the water falls out of the hole?"

Doe nodded, but said nothing.

Miguel hesitated at her silence, then turned to Sam. "Long ago, there were ancient ones that lived on this ranch."

"How long ago?"

"A very long time, *Señor.*"

"Before my people came, they left their place in the cliff up there." Doe spoke in a soft voice, and pointed up at the cliff face.

"They lived in a cave with many rooms . . . like the hotel in Santa Fe."

"Did the Apache live in there?"

She shook her head. "No. It is a place of the dead."

"Uh . . . the grass is strong, *Señor.*" Miguel swallowed, his voice shaky. "The calves are fat, and it cures good. There are many places to water, even in the summer, that are sweet."

It was obvious the *vaquero* loved the place, even if he was a bit on the superstitious side. On the third day out, Miguel parted ways with them and rode off north to the hills. Sam and Doe continued upon the road to Globe.

He looked around. The giant saguaros and palo verde were spaced out across the dry sea of pungent greasewood more graceful than the gray green sage of Colorado. The strong smell filled his nose as Doe rode beside him on the dusty mule.

Manuel Mendoza lived in a two-story frame house in the bustling mining town. The stairs were made of iron and cement and Sam climbed the two flights up to a large carved door. The house looked out of place to him. Far too New England for the southwest desert.

A *señora* politely greeted him.

"Good afternoon, ma'am. I am here to see *Señor* Mendoza. My name is Sam Brennen."

"What is it, Maria?" A man's cultured voice drifted out from the interior.

"A Mister Brennen to see you, sir."

Sam eyed the man, a little taken aback, for the shorter man was dressed much as an eastern businessman without the accent of his Mexican ancestors.

"I do not believe we have met before, Mister Brennen?"

"No, sir. I'm here with a proposal concerning your *hacienda.*"

"The *hacienda*?" The man looked confused. "Oh. You're speaking of my father's cattle ranch up on the mountain. Come in, please."

"It is your ranch?"

"Yes, of course. Do come inside. Would your wife like to come up?" Mendoza gestured toward Doe and the horses out the open door.

"No, thank you. But I would like to speak to you."

Mendoza ushered him inside to a well-appointed parlor. "I hope you have money because I detest that place. Since I went to Harvard, I have only been back there a few times, and my wife hates it there even more

151

than I do."

A woman entered the room from a side door. "Who was it, Manuel?"

The older man gestured for Sam. "Evelyn, my dear, this is Mister Brennen. He wants to discuss the purchase of Father's ranch."

"Well!" The very aloof brunette raised her eyebrows and nodded. Sam decided her piled-up hairdo must have required hours. "I'm certainly interested in hearing this."

"May I fix you a drink?" Mendoza showed him to two fancy chairs and gestured for him to sit.

Sam put his hat on the floor, waving away anyone's offer to take it. "No, thank you, Mister Mendoza. I'm afraid I'm a man of small means, but I'm very interested in the property. Would you tell me what you expect to ask for the place?"

"Oh, a small amount down, and you could pay each year a little payment and some interest."

"How much do you want all together for it?" His heart beat faster, but he wanted to know the total cost.

"I would say . . . oh, perhaps two thousand dollars." Mendoza's hands folded on his chest as he sat back in the chair. "Can you pay half of it down?"

Sam shook his head. "One thousand cash is too high."

"My dear," his wife interrupted, standing beside him. "Since we have not discussed this matter, I hesitate to say that we might discuss a lesser offer to Mister Brennen."

"As you have observed, my wife does not hold my father's ranch in great esteem." His voice was thick with irritation.

"I'm not a rich man." Sam nodded toward the woman wringing her hands around a kerchief. "If you have a good title, I would offer you eight hundred dollars for the ranch and cattle."

"Why, there are hundreds of mother cows on this ranch!"

"Less than a hundred is all I could count." Sam was shaking his head.

"You see, you know more than I do of the place. I rely on an old cowboy who was born on my father's ranch in Mexico to keep the place up."

"Yes, sir."

The woman leaned over and whispered in her husband's ear.

Mendoza listened, his brow furrowed, apparently considering what she had to say. Finally, he waved her away, rubbed his chin, and cleared his throat. "Can you raise that much cash? The eight hundred dollars you mentioned a moment ago?"

"If you give me a day or two, sure. Draw up the papers, and I'll be back to close the deal. Would you like some money down today?"

"It might be best." Mendoza stood and stepped over to a nearby desk as Sam drew five twenty-dollar gold pieces from his pocket. Mendoza wrote a receipt on a stiff slip of parchment paper with a quill pen, then handed it to Sam. They they shook hands.

"Mister Brennen, I must ask you to send Miguel to Globe. He can work as a gardener here in his old age."

"I will tell him. If he wishes, he may also remain at the ranch with me. One more thing . . . does the brand sell in the deal?"

"Of course." Evelyn Mendoza laughed. "What use have we for a brand?"

"Thank you." Sam restored the Stetson to his head.

"Well, now that we've sold the place, perhaps we can move to San Francisco." She smiled. "You see, Manuel is a mining engineer and could work for any firm. There is no need to remain now in this forsaken desert."

Mendoza looked put-out. "Excuse my wife, Mister Brennen. She enjoys the big

154

city life."

"I understand." Sam touched the brim of his hat and nodded to her.

Mendoza shook his hand again as they reached the front door. "I will have the papers in a few days."

Before descending the stairs, Sam put a crestfallen, sober look on his face. On the street, he took the reins silently, and swung into the saddle.

Doe leaned over and peered at his non-telling look. Biting his lip, he shook his head and rode off. Once around the corner, the horses climbed the steep hill street and were soon out of sight of the big house.

Picking their way through the adobe building part of town, Sam turned and laughed. "We didn't buy it. We *stole* it!"

She began giggling. Bent over the saddle-horn, she convulsed in silent laughter, finally bursting out loud. "It took lots of gods, but it worked!"

"Worked?"

She wiped the tears from her eyes. "I have prayed for three days."

"Well, whatever you did, it worked. I have to get hold of our friend up in Prescott. We'll have to send a wire and wait for an answer."

"The ranch house is really ours?"

"Forever and ever — once we sign the papers."

"It is hard to understand how land can be yours when it once belonged to the people. White men have strange ways."

"Yes, we do. We really do." Sam shook his head. "And I wonder how that lawman in Camp Verde could complicate things if he decides to take an interest in us."

"I take care of the horses," she teased, imitating him again.

"Something can be done — I just haven't figured it out."

"You will. You are very lucky." She whistled softly.

Sam frowned. He'd never heard her whistle like that before.

Once they'd sent the wire to the investor in Prescott, they camped on the road north to the mountains to await his reply. They shared a waterhole with a few Mexican women doing laundry for the miners. In the shade of some cottonwood trees, the horses grazed on the sparse, dry, fall forage. Sam purchased enough grain to treat them each evening once they returned to drink at the seeping man-made tank there.

It took two days for Thompson to reply. He could sell the claim for five thousand at present, but if Sam could wait awhile, he

156

felt sure the assay report would help the sale.

Sam folded the paper up and took the pen in hand. He looked down at the blank message slip for a moment, then up at the agent. "Hey, what's the name of the bank down the street?"

"First National," the station agent replied, looking up from his receipts.

"Thanks." Sam wrote out his reply telling Thompson to wait for a better offer and handed it over. Once the station agent started sending it out, he fetched out the coins to pay him.

A short while later, Sam pushed into the steel-barred bank and walked to the first teller window. "Is the president in?"

"Oh, you mean Mister Johnson?" The teller swallowed nervously. "Come this way." He walked behind the caged wall and knocked on a door.

The teller kept glancing nervously back at Sam.

"Excuse me, sir. There's a man out here to see you."

"Send him in, Donagan."

Donagan opened the door for Sam. "Come right back."

Sam introduced himself to the banker and sat in the proffered chair. "I'm buying the

Mendoza ranch and need to put some gold and money in your bank. There's a bank draft coming from my agent, Mister Thompson, in Prescott, that I would like for you to put on interest until I may need it."

"Fine, Mister Brennen, we appreciate your business. Is this Mendoza ranch such a wise investment, though? What with these savages killing and marauding those mountains especially?"

"My mind's made up. I think I'll be all right."

"Well, I do know of some places that are, well, perhaps better ranches."

"Mister Johnson, I barely gave the price of the cows for the old place. Now, I believe confidentiality is a trait in bankers that makes them valuable to depositors."

"Ah." He cleared his throat and searched about as if someone else might be spying on them. "You can trust my absolute secrecy."

"Good. I really think Missus Mendoza — uh, Evelyn — did not covet the old family place."

The banker grinned like he knew the facts. "Really?"

"On the level, I want you to be sure there's no hitch in the title or deal. Hire a lawyer, do what's necessary. I'll cover your

158

expenses."

"Yes, sir, Mister Brennen. And when you're in town, you and the Missus must dine with me at my house."

"How about the Missus Johnson?" Sam wondered if the man knew about Doe, and how his wife might react to her.

"Unfortunately, I lost her some time ago, Mister Brennen. I have observed the woman who rides or rode in . . . Doe Mockingbird? See, I do get the eastern newspaper, too. Come in about seven. Missus Maderas is a great cook and is not afraid of savages."

"How many houses from the Mendozas' house?"

"No, I live much simpler. It is on Phillippe Street. There is a gate in the wall up the hill, pull the bell rope. Someone will answer. Say around seven."

Johnson offered him a cigar offered, and he accepted. Lighting it up, Sam drew slowly, then blew the smoke out. It was strange how good a cigar could taste. Now that the particulars for the ranch were out of the way, he could go about his other business.

"Now let's talk about this." He tossed the gold dust pouch on the desk and placed a pile of money beside it.

Johnson poured the gold flecks carefully

on the shiny balance sheet until the glittering pile rose like a small mountain in the pan. "Are you selling King Solomon's mine, Sam?"

"May have sold it too cheap. Never looked at it since Lady Luck delivered it to me."

"I think you may have. There is well over a thousand dollars here."

"Good deal." Sam drew again on the cigar. "I take it you can get all this accounted for so I can have access to funds when I need them?"

The banker gave a mock bow and bent to start filling out a receipt. "You can rely on me, my good sir."

Later that evening, Sam dismounted at the heavy oak and iron gate and rang the bell. Doe got off the General and looked around. Save for some half-naked children riding a very sleepy burro, the street was deserted.

Johnson welcomed them with a sweeping bow, and a small bent man took their animals, leading them away. Their host led them across the privet-lined courtyard with a festoon of flowers in boxes around the walk.

"Missus Madera," Johnson said with a warm affection, "this is Sam Brennen and Doe Mockingbird."

160

"Good evening. Come with me." The handsome, forty-something woman took Doe warmly by the arm. "These men have bad habits around company."

"Don't spoil her," Johnson warned.

"Oh, heavens, no," came the mock reply. Sam laughed as the tall woman steered Doe toward the house.

"My friends call me Bill, Sam. Now, I have a little — just a little — Kentucky bourbon that they tell me comes from springs of velvet."

"Hmm, that sounds like something downright sinful." Sam laughed as his host poured two glasses of the dark liquid.

"So tell me about the ranch. I've heard about it all my life but never seen it."

"Very nice place we'll have once we get it fixed up. I imagine the house needs some work, but I believe it once was very nice."

The banker was mildly surprised. "You've never been there?"

"No, but Doe has. Once when she was a little girl."

"Little girl, huh? Then she *is* Apache?"

"Yep. Hiding behind the chief's horse's legs. She says she'd never seen such luxury as *Señor* Mendoza had there."

"If you can pack them in, you're welcome to the starts of my flowers. You know there's no road. An ox cart can't get within half a day of the place."

"There's an old Mexican who cares for the place. We met him on the road. He keeps the place for Mendoza."

"Good man, but getting up in age."

"He can show me the ranch, and I learn fast." Sam cleared his throat. "In the meantime, though, I've got another subject I'd like to talk to you about."

"Name it."

"There are some outlaws I need information on."

"Plenty of them around, Sam. Are you still in the bounty business?"

"This is a bit different. Do you know of the Peralta brothers?" Sam finished the bourbon and held out his glass for more.

His host poured in another finger's worth. "We must make one more toast. The men you speak of are a sorry lot of miserable dogs, but I don't know where they are right now."

"You seem to be a man that can get things done. I want to know where they're located. And I'd also like to have five full-blooded Durham bulls to put on those Corrienté cows up at the ranch."

"The bulls aren't a problem. Good ones will be high, but I have a friend in Tucson who has some top stock. Expect them to be here in a month. The Peraltas, though. . . ." Johnson shook his head. "That will take some time. But if the money's there, there are ways to find anyone."

"Bill, a good banker with good whiskey is like a waterhole in the desert." Sam raised his glass. "To our future business relationship."

"To our *successful* business relationship."

"Damn straight. And one day, opportunity will come in your front door, and you'll remember some old brush popper, and we'll partner the deal."

"Indeed I will." Johnson drank to that. "I think Missus Madera has supper ready. Afterwards, we can find some more ideas to spend a fortune on."

Chapter No. 12

Sam and Doe stayed at the Johnson house the rest of the week, closing the land deal and purchasing enough household supplies to last them for a few months at least. Finally, with a pack train of loaded mules and two packers Sam hired in tow, they headed for the ranch.

Doe had to restrain the General, who seemed to sense her excitement as they headed west.

Sam chuckled. "Do you remember the way?"

"I think so, but I will just be happy to be in the mountains again, even if we get lost."

"We won't get lost. We've got more payroll with these mules than I can afford to wander all over."

The second day out, they left the erosion-gouged road and moved down a dim path that swept out between the long mesas through stands barrel cactus, prickly pear, and dry grass. A couple of longhorn cows and calves raised their heads, sniffed the air, and herded their calves nervously away from the strange train. They wore the ranch brand, an M—.

Riding down the long ridge, Sam pointed across the great chasm of live oak to the distant ridge. "See there!"

"It is a strong sign." Doe turned back to look for the train.

"It's a bear. Do you see him?"

She sounded annoyed. "Sam, he can understand what we say."

"Hell, girl, that's just an animal."

"A bear is a powerful spirit. Leave him alone."

The trail wound down from the top of the canyon, sending a few head of longhorns out of the seeping waterhole that seemed to start in a pool and spread over the rocks into another below that one.

Single-file, the train followed along the towering sedimentary bluffs, steeply down into the canyon. They rode through the sandy floor of a dry wash rife with signs of flash floods marring the narrow trail.

He kept an eye on the ridge above where the bear had been, half-amused at her attitude toward the bruin. Shadows were growing deep even in the early afternoon as another canyon came in from the right. A horse-wide trail led up to the east through the chest-high spiny, live oak.

Without hesitation, Doe took the General ahead, and they rode, gaining ground, until they reached a place where they could see the valley ahead.

There, in a valley watered by a spring running down the length and lined with willows, sat a red-roofed *hacienda* between the high-walled cliffs. The spring had once watered the small fields, and they still showed signs of once being irrigated, but neglect to the ditches had left them brown. The stately tamaracks even looked a little pale, but above the wall, they showed the house off.

When Miguel saw them, he leapt from his horse and ran to meet them. "*Señor* Sam! You have come with your *Señora* to live here?"

The yard was brown from lack of water, and dirt had sifted over the tile porch. As Doe held the timber post that supported the porch, she seemed hesitant to enter the open doorway. She swallowed as she inspected the open doorway ahead, half-filled with fear. With slow steps, she crossed the gritty porch.

Miguel apologized. "The house is very

dirty, but if I only knew you would be coming, I would have forgotten the cows and cleaned it."

She turned and hugged the old *vaquero* as tears streamed down her brown cheeks. Miguel cried, too, and held her close while Sam waited patiently for the sadness to pass. At last, he even wiped his own eyes, and then moved on past the pair.

Doe swallowed and released the man, then hurried to catch up.

The house *did* need repairs, but its elegance was there. Sam slipped his arm over her shoulder as they cautiously inspected their new home. The furniture, in particular was in desperate need of replacement, and the house appeared inhabited by a great population of pack rats. Each room hung deep in cobwebs and stale dust that proved ready to fly when the large plank doors were pushed in with an eerie squeak.

Doe laughed, whirling the skirt out and bowing like some debutante she saw one time in a book. "This will be a great place for you, Sam Brennen."

"For *us!* This whole place is for *us!*"

"It is so great. Could we afford it?"

"Joe Sunday gave us this for a wedding present."

"Oh." She stopped, crestfallen and bowed

her head.

"Hey." He pried up her sad face and kissed her nose gently. "You and I *will* be married. Don't listen to the law in Camp Verde. Here, we *are* the law!"

"I would rather tend the horses all my life than for you to be lost from me."

"That we'll cross that bridge when we get there."

"Where is Miguel?"

"On the porch."

"Then let's go talk to him."

Their new friend was waiting for them, hat in hand.

"This place needs lots of work, but we like it." Sam hugged the resistant Doe under his arm.

Miguel nodded. "*Señor,* there are some cousins of mine in Casa Grande who would love to come back here where they were born when *Señor* Mendoza was here. They are good farmers and carpenters, and their families would help us fix this place up."

"How many would come?" Sam screwed up his face.

"There is Pedro and Marie, and they have children. José and Lena, and they have some children, and if you would let me also bring Juan, Margarita, and their family. . . . *Señor,* we would make this place look like it did

168

when we were young."

"How many children?"

"Oh, I don't know. Too many?"

"How soon before your daughter is a teacher?"

The older man's face lit up. "Next year."

"We better plan on a school here."

"Oh, that would be very nice."

"How will that many people get here?" Doe asked.

"Pack train, I guess," Sam said, a little undecided.

"There are some burros on Wild Horse Mesa that were once broke. And some horses on the Rio Salado."

"Good, let's get these packers sent home, and we'll go try our luck at mustanging." Sam stretched as he finished speaking. What a wonderful secret place they'd found.

In the morning, the packers shook his hand.

One said, "I'll be glad to get home in my bed. This old place is sure something, but I'd rather keep my scalp."

Sam nodded and hugged Doe beside him. "Fellows, be careful."

"We will." They waved and headed out. As they rode down the overgrown path, Sam and Doe went to find their own mounts. To their surprise, Miguel had the mare and

General Crook already saddled.

They rode out what Miguel called the "back way" and climbed out of the canyon on a narrow trail only fit for the sure-footed or a mountain goat.

"There are two horse trails in and out, and two for the brave on foot," Miguel explained as their horses topped out on the grassy greasewood hills. The occasional century plant stalk dotted the land, its life spent to flower once, a brown stiff stalk marked its death.

"Have you ever used the *reata?*" Miguel asked.

"No, but I can swing a rope. Is it harder?" Sam pointed to the hand-braided fine leather lasso of the *vaquero.*

Miguel handed it over. "You will never use the rope again."

"Then a *reata* is what I shall use." Sam deftly dropped the loop over a rock and dallied around the horn. The mare instinctively turned and tightened the rope. He laughed. "I think this lady has been used on cattle before."

The burros Miguel had mentioned were scattered throughout a small ravine. They hardly lifted their heads at the approaching riders. Then they saw The General. Braying, at the top of their lungs, the suddenly they began to approach the larger mule.

Doe's eyebrows rose and she giggled. The smile on her face was radiant. "I think they may have found a new leader."

"Get your rope ready."

Sam roped the first fuzzy burro. He had the marks of a saddle on his back. Captured, the animal barely fought as Sam snubbed him up. Miguel roped another, and it tried to buck. Only his quick spur turned his big roan and he rode off just in time to avoid being kicked by two sharp hind feet. Whipping the burro over the butt with his quirt subdued the thick-maned donkey and reminded it of man's power from its past.

Haltering the first two, they managed to catch two more easily, and the others moved off, acting more elusive.

His spurs jabbing the mare to make her go faster, Sam leaned in the saddle, the fine rawhide coil swishing over his head as the next burro in line flattened his ears and ducked his head. The loop fell true, and the burro, realizing he was captured, ran backwards. Sam gritted his teeth and wrapped the rope around the horn, snubbing the little mount up short.

Miguel roped another spooked one and was having to keep up with its wild antics. Darting behind his new Segundo's roan caused the rope to goose it into a crow hop that made Doe laugh out loud.

"This burro hunting is sure fun." Doe grinned, jumping off to halter Sam's catch. She ducked a pair of flashing donkey teeth, joked about his age, and soon had him haltered.

Before noon, they had rounded up a dozen of the small beasts of burden and were headed back to the *hacienda*.

Doe's face beamed with excitement. "I think we will have fun at this place."

Sam laughed in agreement. "First day, and we have our own mule train."

"You've roped before," Miguel noted.

"Sure, but it was a long time ago."

"You learn well."

"Roping burros and roping Corrienté cows is a lot different."

"We will see."

Doe rode in close. "What do you think now?"

Oh, this is more than I ever imagined." He clapped her on the leg. "And this, my dear, is just the beginning."

"Do you promise?"

Sam winked and tipped his hat. "Always."

CHAPTER No. 13

Early the next morning, Miguel started out for Casa Grande. With a wide grin, he rode out leading the shaggy string of captured burros nodding along behind. If a person could shed years, he had surely lost a half century off his age.

With her broom of stiff grass, Doe began the job of sweeping the place out. As the dust flew this way and she moved to the next room, Sam labored along behind her hauling buckets of water to slosh down on the tile floors. Mopping with the vengeance of an angry woman, Doe attacked the accumulation dirt of years of neglect.

Late in the day, Sam swept her up off her feet, and the mop flew sloppily off. Carrying her in his arms, he took her into the bedroom and dumped her into the feather-bed she'd restored from its abandoned state the night before.

Nuzzling her face, he sprawled beside her

and closed his eyes to savor their moment together.

Doe closed her eyes and settled deep in the canyon of the feather mattress. Her full lips parted, and she began to breathe deeply. As easily as a summer storm can gather where there was nothing once but blue skies, the great thunderheads of passion rose, and the winds of the storm was their breath as they sought the height of eagles. Then, like the crash of thunder, they plunged into darkness and the stillness of the damp afterwards.

"Sam?"

"Yeah?"

"Is it like this with white women?"

He snorted. "Nothing is ever the same. Some are. Some aren't. You and I are very special together."

"Good." She sounded satisfied.

A couple of days later, they rode to Globe for more supplies. Before heading for the mercantile, though, they stopped at the bank, and Bill came out to meet them.

"Go on up to the house, Doe, and tell Missus Madera that her favorite rancher is here for supper."

Sam waved him off. "We can put ourselves up."

"Go on, Doe." He grinned and shooed her on. "You're staying at my place, and that's that."

Sam dismounted and shook his head. "I may go to Phoenix next time."

"Not after you hear what I have to tell you." Seated in his office, Bill began. "Your agent, Mister Thompson, sent you a five-hundred-dollar draft and an agreement with the Acme Mining Co. Seems that they're willing to pay you the balance and ten percent of the mine's net profit over the next ten years. The balance of some ten thousand dollars . . . of which Mister Thompson is going to hold out two thousand for his services."

"Are you serious?" Sam frowned, amazed.

"Yes. I am."

"Well, my Lord, that is beyond belief!"

"You also have a letter from the Judge in Colorado on my desk. The one you wrote before you left."

"Sounds like I have to hire me a secretary."

"Oh, and you should get delivery on those red Durham bulls sometime in the winter."

Awed by things happening so fast, Sam opened the letter from the judge and scanned it quickly.

Dear Sam,

There has been no word of the man you are seeking. I have checked with the Denver police, but he must have departed there, for they intensified their patrols looking for him. Hoping this letter finds you in good health. I did read where you were collecting bounties with an Indian woman. You are fast becoming a legend.

Sincerely Your Honorable,
Walter H. Miller

"Any news?" Bill asked.

Sam gazed out the window. Damn. Another dead end. His life had many of them — when things looked good, something else always seemed to come along to smother them.

"Sam?" the banker pushed.

"No, Bill. No lead on the man I'm looking for. He's moved on, and I guess may never surface."

"The man?"

"Three men killed my wife and two daughters back in Colorado. I found two of 'em — Doe and I did — and they'll never hurt another soul. The third one's still loose, though. I got close to him once, but he got away."

"Oh," Bill said slowly. "I'm sorry."

"Me, too." Sam was quiet for a moment. "I guess I'm making a pretty poor avenger. It looks like it's over."

Bill got up and came around the desk. "Maybe you don't need to be an avenger at all anymore, Sam. You've got a lot of good things going on, and a lot of good you can do here. With me and Doe."

He looked up. "You think so?"

"I do, indeed. In fact, I have another deal for you to consider right now?"

"What kind of deal?"

"I have a man with a sawmill that needs money and partners. Late Emery is a good man, but he's very short on capital. He was in last week, and I mentioned that the two of us might be interested in the lumber."

"How much?"

"Your part, two or three thousand when the mine deal comes through."

"Do it. I can scrape up that much in old coins if you can quietly work them into the money supply."

"Old coins?"

He shrugged. "Some outlaws willed me some. They weren't from any reported crime, but they're all Mexican gold."

"Hey, maybe you dug it up on the ranch."

"Maybe. There are some jealous, nosy people out there, though."

"Leave the money to me, my friend." Bill clapped him on the shoulder. "That's my business."

Sam slumped in the chair. *Business.* He sighed. The need to move forward — to do *something* — rather than focusing on the ghosts of Colorado was all but overwhelming. But money and business deals did nothing to cover the ache of failure to deliver justice for his dead family. "Anything else?"

"One more, and we're going to the house, okay?"

"Fine, what is that?"

"I think I have a man who knows where the Peralta brothers are at."

Now *that* perked him up. "Where?"

"South of Tucson. On a ranch of the fellow who no doubt benefits from their persistence."

Sam stood. "I want the location."

"Don't worry, I'll get it." Bill lowered his voice. "But why the Peraltas?"

"They killed a young Indian girl's mother, raped the child, and sold her into slavery."

"Doe?"

"I owe those two sons of bitches the same kind of pain they made her suffer through." He looked up. "And I aim to pay that debt."

Bill met his gaze and nodded. "I understand."

After a moment of silence, Sam cleared his throat. "One more problem I need solved, Bill. This law here in Arizona about an Indian marrying a white man being a felony."

Bill shrugged. "The penitentiary in Yuma would be full if they actually enforced it."

"I don't want trouble, but I do want a legal marriage with her."

"I have a good lawyer. We'll let him figure out where to begin on that. Do I have some time?"

"Yes." Sam was satisfied Bill would find a solution for him.

Johnson's home was a quiet reprieve from the noisy streets of Globe. Missus Madera was the usual bright hostess, and the evening passed very pleasantly over spicy food and lively conversation. Afterward, Sam and Bill retired to the library to smoked cigars and sip bourbon.

"Sam Brennen, you hardly seem the usual type to be a lawman."

"What's usual? I was raised in Missouri on a good farm. My father owned a store where I clerked 'til I was nineteen. I got a wild notion and went to Texas, worked cattle drives up north to Kansas. While I was there, I got hired as a deputy in Wichita, married a very good woman with two small girls, and went up to Fort Collins to do more law work. One night that dream ended in a bloody nightmare. I started looking for three killers. I got lost and drunk. I met Joe Sunday. He shot my horse, in turn, I shot him and inherited Doe, all in that same day." Sam's lips compressed and he slumped some in his chair. "That's my story. What about you?"

"My father built this bank. He came here from Illinois and sent me to school. Then one day, he fell over from a heart attack. The woman I married died in childbirth. Missus Madera lost her husband in a mine accident. So . . . well, it's a nice arrangement we have."

Sam raised his glass. "She is a gracious hostess."

"Everything I need." Johnson took a drink of his whiskey.

"Oh, I nearly forgot." He laughed. "Miguel's gone to Casa Grande to get his cousins and, oh, a few wives and children."

"What?"

"We plan to make the *hacienda* look like when *Señor* Mendoza was here." He mimicked the *vaquero*. The banker laughed, doubling over in hysterics. "Oh, Bill, you should have seen the burro round up. We sent the old man off with the wildest looking pack string you could imagine."

"Good! You'll have that place shaped up in no time."

"Tell me one thing. How did Mendoza ever build that place without a road up there?"

"He built it all up there. Brought the craftsmen with him from Mexico. I've never been there, but they tell me that's how he did it."

An hour or so later, the two men finally wound down and said there good evenings. Sam joined Doe in the spacious guest bedroom and they slept in one another's arms.

For a little while, at least.

Unable to sleep, he left Doe sleeping in the bed and walked down the hall into the courtyard in the early morning darkness. A cold north wind blew chilly over the open flower garden. There was frost in the air. Protected, the boxes of flowers seemed to be cheerful as they swayed in the drafts that swept in the courtyard. The stars were still out as Sam stood in his shirtsleeves, hugging his arms for warmth.

"*Señor,* come in the kitchen. There is coffee."

The voice startled him. He turned to find Missus Madera standing in the yellow-lighted kitchen, looking at him through the open door.

"Thanks." Sam grinned as he ducked going into the warm kitchen. Taking the coffee, he leaned against the wall and blew great vapors of steam off the surface.

"You do not sleep good in this house?"

"Sleep?" He shook his head. "Oh, I sleep fine, just woke up with things on my mind."

"*Señor* Johnson says you have been very successful in your business. Or do you simply worry as he does?"

"Does he worry?" Sam looked over his coffee at the attractive, buxom woman. She was in her early forties, perhaps five years or so older than Bill. Dark eyes, a full mouth, and the beautiful impeccable olive complexion of her ancestors.

She smiled. "Oh, only all the time."

"How did you get here?"

"It's not a very long or dramatic story." A shrug. "My husband was killed in a mine accident ten years ago. We had borrowed money from the bank to buy a small house. When my husband died, I had no way to pay it back. Washing clothes would never repay the loan. Bill needed a housekeeper, so I sold the house and came here."

"He never offered to marry you?" Sam studied the red chilies drying on the wall.

He had a hunch as to how this story would end.

"He would, but you do not understand the politics of banking. When you run a bank, you do not marry a Mexican housekeeper and expect to keep the *gringo* business."

"I figured as much. You're secure here as the housekeeper, and you only call him Bill when your guard is down." Sam grinned as she looked up at him in surprise. "I'll have some more coffee."

"I shall have to watch myself more carefully, Mister Brennen." She raised her shoulders and looked very much the dignified housekeeper.

"The secret is locked in me." She held out a fresh doughnut and he took it. "Teach Doe how to cook those, and I'll end up fatter than an old *patron.*"

"You'd be surprised." She led him into the dining room.

He agreed with a nod and ambled along behind her.

"Are you trying to steal my cook, too?" Bill looked up sleepy-eyed from his chair at the great oak table.

Sam looked at him archly. "Her *and* her recipes."

"You can't have her. The recipes, okay,

but not her."

"Perhaps you ought to consider changing her name so no one tries?"

She frowned at him. "Mister Brennen. . . ."

"Missus Madera, I simply think that you two ought to . . . *reconsider* your little arrangement."

"Perhaps we should," Bill agreed.

"Say, we're friends, and both of us have a similar problem. Don't we both need a solution?"

"I'm pleased to be where I am. As a housekeeper." She turned and hurried out of the room.

Sam looked over at his friend. "Sorry I mentioned it. I hope I haven't caused you any trouble."

"No, you've hit the nail on the head. It's time to be honest with one's self and the ones you love."

"You could do a helluva lot worse — no matter where you picked one."

Bill looked up as Doe appeared in the doorway. She nodded cordially at her host and gestured to Sam. "Sometimes he does not sleep. I have to go looking for him at dawn to make sure he hasn't run off in the night."

Bill laughed. "Juanita?"

184

"Yes?" Her face appeared.

"This morning seems to be some kind of very messed up deal. Bring in the doughnuts, would you? And let's laugh at something."

"Good." She smiled and brought forth a heaping plate of doughnuts.

CHAPTER NO. 14

Sam and Doe rode back to the ranch the next day. Two wagons of goods were to be delivered to the end of the road in one week. Sam decided Miguel and his train would surely be back by then. There was barley to seed in the fields — once they could be irrigated, that is — farming tools, rope, nails, wire, and carpenter tools.

A wild wind swept dust across the desert floor around them. Dark high clouds that promised rain forced them to pull their rain gear loose from behind their saddles as they leaned into the freshening breeze. Soon muddy drops pelted them and slowed their progress along the dim little road, skirting the erosive ditches from previous downpours. The air, cleaned of the dirt, had the strong smell of greasewood.

Frequent, distant thunder rolled across Iron Mountain as they crossed over the pass and started down the long canyon trailing the gray rain. Reaching the gate, Sam heard the burros bray, and General Crook answer.

Doe searched Sam's face in the rivers of rain streaming off the brim of his hat. "Our family is here!"

"I reckon so!"

When they reached the corrals, Sam started to unsaddle the horse and mule, but two men rushed out and took them, instead, tying them to the hitch rail and showing them to the security of the porch.

On the wide veranda, in a faded gold vest under a giant tasseled *sombrero,* his boots oiled bright, stood Miguel. He hugged Sam and swept the giant hat off to the polished tile floor for Doe. "*Señor,* the burros told us you were coming."

Sam turned to see the large line of assembled people. The entire group bowed and smiled as Miguel introduced each one, including the children and did a good job with the names. Sam decided he would learn them with time.

When the *vaquero* finished his introductions, Sam smiled. "Welcome back home. Your home and our home. We will raise our families and fix this great *hacienda* into the place you remember. There is not much money, but we will eat good, and there will be a school, and we will be happy."

A roar went up from the small crowd. With a flourish, Miguel escorted them into a completely clean house. Sam hugged Doe under his arm as he propelled her along with him.

A giant feast had been laid on, and a great new table, polished smooth by talented hands, filled the dining room. An ancient chair with a high back was at the end, and a lesser carved oak one sat at the table head. Benches were lined along the table, cruder than the rest but no doubt hastily made for the occasion.

"I hope you do not dislike our work, but we wanted to surprise you." Miguel looked proudly for approval from the waiting crowd.

Doe hugged him and, taking off the wet Stetson with deliberate grace, raised her head and smiled. "Welcome to our *hacienda.* All of you."

"We are very pleased." Sam nodded and hugged her as she finished her short speech. "Be seated."

They were like ants scurrying around the valley. The irrigation system was repaired, and the farming tools were packed in from the end of the road. The cold of winter nights and warm sunny days that heated the valley allowed the barley to sprout and green up from the once-barren fields.

Miguel, Sam, and Doe had checked the cattle, branding mavericks on the range. Using the bald-faced horse, Sam would sweep in and rope the longhorns while the older man caught their heels, stretching them out. Doe carried the branding iron from the glowing fire and administered the mark. Once this was done, they moved on to the next item on the list — castration. Castration of the longhorn bulls was an important process if the Durham bulls were to improve the stock. Miguel had overlooked many before to provide the needed manhood to produce more calves.

Sam rode down into a ravine swinging the rope, when a thick-horned heavy-necked male turned back to charge. There was nowhere to go, but in such a confined space, the bull couldn't use all his strength. Still, he managed to knocked over the sorrel easily, pinning Sam under the horse against the bank of the ravine. Hooking and butting the horse only added to the pain as Sam reached for his empty holster. Somehow his gun had jolted loose in the crash and was somewhere beneath the marauding brute. Raging in his deep voice, the bull slashed the air with horns that had crossed the

Mediterranean Sea with the Moors who invaded Spain.

The sorrel horse screamed in pain as the bull battered both horse and rider in the narrow confines of the wash. A shot rang out, and another, and the bull fell with a thud. The rifle's report echoed across the mountains. The sorrel horse struggled off his injured rider, shaking himself until the stirrups popped, then running off. Dragging his left leg, Sam caught the reins, then collapsed to the ground.

"Sam, you all right?" Doe slid down the mountain side on the General.

She tried to boot the rifle in the scabbard, but couldn't hit it right. Finally, she shoved it half in and left it there. Out of breath, she rushed through the sandy wash to him. Miguel, who had been hazing in another bull, came riding in as fast as his cowpony could go.

Sam was on his back, holding the reins and feeling the damaged leg through his pants. He shook his head. "Looks like I've really done it now."

"Is it bad?" She slid in front of him, dropping down to feel the leg.

He groaned through gritted teeth. "Just get me on the horse."

She ignored him and examined the leg

with her hands. "Be still."

"Doe, get me on the damn horse. I don't aim to ride home in a *travois.*"

"Be still. You could make it worse."

Sam ignored her. The damn leg was going to swell. He wanted in the saddle and back at the house before the pain killed him. "Miguel, give me a hand and get me on the horse, now!"

"No!" She tried to fight them, but Sam was up and hobbling toward the horse. She jerked the mule around to mount him. "You damn men! Go to hell."

"Lead out, Doe. We need to get home." Sam swallowed his pain. Miguel helped him into the saddle, and he bit down on another moan. Holding the saddlehorn, he felt the sorrel limping as they moved southwest across the mesa.

He had to make it back to the house. He simply had to. The pain in his left leg was throbbing as he hung it out of the stirrup.

Doe reined the mule back beside him and searched his taut face. "Are you going to make it?"

"Sure." Sam tried not to show her the mounting sharpness. "I'm sorry, but we just need to ride."

"You are stubborn as this mule, but I am sorry you are hurt." She moved ahead so he

191

did not have to pretend it was okay for her. Miguel rode behind her. Sam squeezed his burning leg with his hand and then had to let it back down beside the stirrup. Closing his eyes against the knife-like ache, he leaned forward to try to escape it.

After an hour, he hollered for them to stop. Breathing hard, he waved Miguel up to beside his horse.

"We've got to pull the boot off. It's swelling, and I don't want to cut the damn thing off."

Miguel nodded, knelt and gently pulled on the scuffed Kansas-made boot. Looking up at Sam, he questioned how bad it was going to hurt him. The boot was coming off very hard, and the effort was forcing Sam to suck in his breath. Finally, the boot began to slide, and Miguel gave a quick start as he saw the swollen ankle in the sock ooze out of the vamp.

"You can't ride in with that," Doe protested, half crying.

"I'm tough as any Apache. Get on your mule," he spit through his teeth.

Was he? He would tell her when he couldn't make it. Pain began shooting into his hip as he clung to the horn. His world grew dizzier as they descended into the canyon, and Sam could barely see his horse's ears.

The words that they spoke to him, he only grunted back.

The horse seemed to wobble under him as he clung to the horn with both hands half-way unconscious as bolts like thunder flashed through his whole body.

He couldn't remember the gentle, strong arms that carried him from the horse to the feather bed.

Stripped of his clothes, Margarita examined the swollen limb and decided it was not broken. She and Doe applied cool packs to it as Sam tossed in a half-sleep and alternated between chilling and sweating. Once in a half-dream, he heard himself screaming. "Why did they kill you, Alicia? Why? Why? Why did they ruin my life?"

Margarita looked at Doe for an answer.

"His first wife, they kill her. Very bloody. It is the thing that eats him, the last one has not been punished."

"Oh, my." The woman who would serve as the doctor for this remote place was intent on relieving the swelling.

"Doe," he mumbled. "Who is this crazy horse-shooter?"

"It's all right, Sam." She pressed her forehead to his cheek.

The next morning, he seemed better to

the two women as he stirred, grabbing for his knee. "Did Miguel cut that damn thing's throat?"

Doe sleepily shook her head. "He did that. They are already on their way to see if they can salvage the meat."

"I need to. . . ."

"Crazy man, lay down. They are not stupid. You have been out of your head all night. You are **not** getting out of bed."

"Yes, ma'am." He heard the irritation in her voice and laid back down. "But if Margarita will leave, I'll swing out of bed for a minute, or you'll have more problems. . . ."

Margarita nodded and left the room.

He realized then how swollen the left leg was. In a while, Doe went out into the hall and called to her as breakfast came on a tray from the kitchen.

"Doe, somewhere there's some whiskey in this place. I reckon I'm going to need some if I am going to stand this thing."

She nodded and swept out of the room, noticing that he was only playing at eating. Sam sipped the coffee and squirmed on his rump, trying to find a place the leg hurt less. The whiskey that the search party finally found numbed his mind enough that he finally dozed off, but awoke sharply when he moved the injured limb.

The second day, with a crutch, he moved onto the porch when the sun got high enough to warm the tiles. Doe looked very tired as he sat in the chair beside her, the leg on a bench to hold it rigid.

"One who does not sleep, better go take a *siesta.* Go on. I'll be okay. Besides, there are ten thousand people who would come lift my little finger if I needed help."

"Are you sure?"

"You heard the *patron.*" He laughed.

She giggled, sounding relieved. "Well, the *patron* better behave, or I'll scalp him."

"Man alive, who in the world would ever keep a bloodthirsty Apache around for a house kitten?"

"No, *you* have a mountain lion." She rose from her chair, smiled, and walked away.

Chapter No. 15

For Sam, the cold days of winter, shortened by the sun's journey south, seemed to last forever. He wondered how late in the year it was and remembered it would surely soon be Christmas. He sent for Miguel, who had not been around that day.

"Miguel, when will it be Christmas?"

"In a week, *Señor*."

"Good Lord, man, take the pack horses and go to Phoenix. See your daughter and get some oranges and some pecans. Oh, and plenty of candy for the kids . . . and have your daughter pick out some bolts of material for dresses, thread and needles for the women."

"*Sí, Señor,* anything else?"

"Yes, you buy that girl of yours some new dresses. I want the school marm of this *hacienda* to be proud of all the folks who are waiting for her."

"You are a generous man."

"Foolish, too. Now, get going, we don't want to miss Christmas." He pushed up and hobbled on the crutch beside his *Segundo.*

Less than an hour later, Miguel was mounted up and riding off with the pack horses and money.

Doe came in with a frown. "Where is Miguel going?"

"To get supplies." Sam grinned foolishly from his chair by the fireplace.

"Supplies?"

"For Christmas."

"What did you send him after?"

"Surprises." Sam looked back at the fireplace.

She shook her head and left the room.

He studied the fire as burning oak cracked and sputtered. Lifting his still-sore leg, he stretched his aching back muscles, tense from the lack of activity. The place was taking shape, and the people were industrious and always smiled for him. Everyone appeared so anxious to restore the place that even the little children worked in between childish games. Little girls damp-mopped the tile floors under the stern eye of Margarita each day. She quieted them with a short shush if they became too loud to her ears. Doe and the girls in the kitchen always managed to turn out dishes that varied the *frijoles* diet. Miguel shot a deer once a week, and that provided venison.

Sam noted they had jerked a steer as well as the angry bull. If his *Segundo* found a dead cow, he always brought the hide back. Rawhide was a valuable part of the things they needed, from sandals to saddle repair.

A few winter vegetables were mixed in the fields that produced as the men established plots. They were constantly hauling the horse barn excrement and spreading it on the fields with carts they made. When they weren't out chopping firewood on the mountain, they brought loads of sun-cured grass for hay on the burros that dwarfed the little shaggy fellows.

He hit his upper leg with his palm, angry over the slow healing process.

"What is wrong now?" Doe sat down beside him offering doughnuts.

"My stupid leg." Then he smiled. "No, we haven't got much time to get ready for Christmas, either."

"I thought it was a white man's deal."

"I'm sorry." He patted her arm, nodding with understanding as he took a doughnut.

"I never knew what Christmas was until I came to the mission. I guess Indians had no such thing, but we did have dances. I wish that I could go to those dances again."

198

"If they still have dances, we will go if they will allow me."

"I do not want to go if you could not come."

"Miguel is getting all the things I remember having when we had Christmas at my house."

"Oh, that will be nice."

"Wait till you see all those little kids' faces. They work like the devil around here."

"I shall wait to see those little faces." She gave him a wink and left to oversee her kitchen.

Sam had ordered the big juniper that the men set up in the main room. Hopping around on his crutches, he had to be everywhere, swinging a crutch to point things out. Doe watched him from a distance shaking her head, amused.

Miguel arrived with the pack horses loaded, and Sam made it at breakneck speed on his crutches to meet the weary but pleased *Segundo.*

"Margarita, you and Lois are in charge of hiding all this for Christmas. Doe will help. Miguel, let's sit by the fire. I must hear how our schoolteacher is. What news do you have from her?"

"*Señor,* oh, the dresses are lovely, and she

199

sends her best. She wanted to come back here for Christmas, but the people where she stays needed her. There is plenty of candy and plenty of fruit. Oh, and she picked out the material. I did not forget one thing. I was afraid that I had too much on the horses, but they made it okay. How is your leg?"

"Fine, fine. Here, drink some good whiskey." Sam was almost unable to sit still.

"It will be a fine Christmas, *Patron*. This will be greater than any this hacienda ever had."

"Miguel, we will always have the merriest Christmases on the ranch."

The house was astir. Youngsters were dashing about excited on Christmas Eve. Sam told Doe he could not wait.

The juniper was decorated with strings of popcorn and carved animals some of the men had made. Their homemade decorations were delightful.

The noise was almost ear-shattering, and Sam hobbled after Doe who was heading down the hall.

"Is everybody ready?" he yelled, out of breath on his crutches.

"Oh, Sam, it is going to be so exciting. You have so many nice things for everyone. You must have spent a fortune."

"Doe, Christmas is special, and these people have done a special job for us."

"It will be. Miguel is coming." She looked troubled.

"*Patron,* excuse me. But there is a problem outside." Miguel sounded very concerned. "A . . . big problem."

"What is it?"

"There are several Apaches — men, women, and children — in the yard."

"What do they want?"

"I think they are starving, *Patron.*"

"Doe, let's go speak to them."

"Yes." She fell in beside him as he hobbled on his crutches.

The main room was very quiet, and he noticed the ranch men were all armed. They appeared to be waiting for his word about what to do.

Sam paused and made a stay inside sign, then he and Doe went out the front. Sam noticed first it was cold out there in the dark compared to inside the house. They stood there, the leader wrapped in his blanket, another short man stood beside him, behind them was an older gray-haired man. There were about six women and four small children.

"What do you want?" Doe asked them in her halting Apache.

"The winter is cold. It is a long way back to Camp McDowell. We are without food or ammunition."

Sam caught the name of the army camp west on the Verde, but the rest was unintelligible to him.

Doe asked again. "What do you want here?"

"Once my father's people came here for a treaty."

"You were not here for that!" Her voice was full of anger.

The leader was displeased with her response. "How come the man does not talk?"

"I am his woman, and he does not speak the language."

"What do they want?" Sam kept his voice quiet.

"They are beggars, not men! They plead for the old treaty the Apaches made with Mendoza."

"What should we do?"

"Send them away! They are reservation dogs! They are without pride. They were not here when Natise made the treaty. They eat government meat. Let them walk back there and eat."

"It's four days to Camp McDowell or more, Doe." He eyed the Indians as he spoke under his breath. "They might not make it."

"These are not the same people who made the treaty."

"Doe, what did the *padre* tell you about Christmas?"

"Christmas is for children." Her silence was long. "These are just pitiful beggars out here in this cold."

"Invite them inside, Doe."

Raising to her full height, she spoke to them. "This is a time of big dance for these people when they feast and sing and give gifts because of a great God that was born. You must be polite, and if one thing is missing, my man would put to death the thief. You must eat slowly, even if they do not know how in the way of these people."

A small child ran forward and hugged her legs. It was very quiet as the December wind swept off the distant snowy Four Peaks across the mountains. Reaching down, she took the child's hand, and the others followed as the sound of Spanish Christmas carols began inside. The Apaches seemed blinded by the splendor but sat at attention on the far side of the great room like an island as Doe indicated.

"We are here to celebrate, and these people are without a place to celebrate. We are very fortunate to have so much, and we will share it with the less fortunate. They can do no harm to us. Doe has asked them to be here."

Relief came over the people in the great room. Sam hobbled over to the great chair and spoke to Margarita. She nodded, and with some of the older children, went after some food for the Apaches. As the caroling continued, Sam smiled at the way they ate despite the fact they were very hungry.

"Are they too weak to eat?"

"No! I told them how to act or you would kill them." She gave him a knowing wink.

"Miguel, bring a chair, and sit here. You know everybody's name, and you will give out the presents."

"But *Patron,* that is your job." Miguel donned his gold-braided vest for the occasion.

"No way! These people you have gathered have resurrected this ranch, and Doe and I are very proud, but you told us this was a great ranch, and it is becoming one. It is our great present from you all."

"You make me too proud for this vest. I think my heart will break."

"It won't, I promise! Get on before the children get too sleepy to enjoy their presents."

"Si, patron."

The gifts were in cotton sacks that made the children's eyes bug at the size. Smiling, they thanked the *Segundo* and nodded at the smiling pair who sat back. Margarita whispered in Sam's ear, and he nodded as Doe turned and looked at Sam with a frown.

"She has some things she held back for the Apache children."

Doe nodded in agreement as the woman handed oranges and handfuls of candy to the visitors. Each nodded and looked at the others in bewilderment at the thing they least expected.

The man who led them rose and cleared his throat. Silence fell upon the room as the Apache spoke in English. "We have heard of this man Jesus and surely he must be a good god. We are grateful to you, even if we cannot repay you. We will leave now."

"The rascal can speak English," Sam said under his hand.

"I did not know that," she whispered back.

"Tell them they are welcome to sleep on our floor and may leave whenever they choose."

Doe looked at him in disgust. "He can understand English. You tell him!"

Later in the night, Sam and Doe lay in their

featherbed. Still elated with the spirit of the holiday, Sam found himself unable to sleep. Nestled half on top of him in her nightgown, she kept smiling in the yellow candlelight.

"Did you ever have a Christmas like this when you were a boy?"

"Not this big, but they were good times. The first Christmas I spent away from home was in an old leaky line shack with two old cowboys who gave each other their own pocketknives as presents. Guess the next year they did the same thing over again."

"Did you see the children's faces?"

"I saw one wide-eyed child hug your skirt on the porch."

"Sam Brennen!" She pounded him on the chest with her fist. "I have daydreamed of returning to my people to see the dances, the big celebrations. I can remember the days of Natise. They were proud people. We did not come here to beg from Mendoza."

"Nothing is ever the same except the sun." Sam hugged her to himself. Quietly, her warm tears fell on his bare chest.

With the morning, their visitors had left. It was still cold outside.

Felize Navidad, Patron." Miguel put wood in the fireplace.

"Merry Christmas, Miguel. Our friends left?"

"*Sí, Señor.* We sent food with them for their trip back to Camp McDowell."

"Good." Sam nodded in approval.

"It's strange about them. Once we all would have feared the Apache. Last night, we were sorry for them — they were barefooted and so hungry."

"Don't mention it to Doe. She was very upset about it."

The *Segundo* nodded in understanding and straightened up. Rubbing his sun-squinted eyes, the *vaquero* leaned against the fireplace and absorbed the radiant heat. "Is your leg better?"

"I think so." Sam stared at the flames as they licked up in the air and consumed the dry wood.

"Is something wrong?"

"Miguel, I'm very pleased with the things I can do something about, but there are things that are left undone, not here, but in my life."

"If I can be of service. . . ."

"No, these are some thing I have to do . . . myself."

"We all would help."

"I know. Tomorrow I want the mare and the General saddled. We need to go to Globe for business and may need to be gone for a while."

Sam and Doe left in the early light, riding the canyon, wrapped warm in blanket coats in the chill and deep shadowy darkness. Sam's leg was still sore, but after a few hours in the saddle, it began to get worse. He shifted his weight occasionally, trying to find a more comfortable position.

Doe noticed him flopping around and shook her head in disapproval. "You want to go back?"

"No, I'll be okay." He raised up on his good leg in the stirrup.

She pushed the shotgun down in its boot under her right leg and frowned. There was no doubt that she couldn't change his mind. No reason to feel sorry for anyone that stubborn, but she did.

The copper-colored mare was well enough broke that you could dismount her on the right as well as the left. They rested in a dry wash out of the cold wind, and Sam stood as they ate the lunch Margarita had sent.

Washing it down with water from the canteen, he shook his head. "I need some whiskey."

"I think so, too." She shook her head and looked through his saddlebags. Handing him the bottle, she watched him uncork it and drink from the neck.

With a shudder, he popped the cork in.

"Let's ride before I become a bigger baby."

She helped him back up on the mare with him still carrying the whiskey bottle in his off hand. Slowly, he swung aboard with a false smile of gratitude as he settled in the saddle.

They had finally made it to the military road and had passed a freight wagon headed for Globe when shots rang out ahead.

With a nod of his head, Sam gave the mare her lead, pulling the Winchester out as he rode. He saw two men robbing a stage coach maybe a quarter-mile ahead.

He motioned for Doe to go left. She swept off on the mule into the greasewood and disappeared. Riding closer, Sam fired the Winchester once into the air over his head to announce his presence. "Hold it!"

Surprised by his sudden appearance, the robbers forgot their intended victims and bolted for their horses.

The mare was closing the gap. One of the outlaws, holding the reins of his wide-eyed horse, turned and fired his pistol at Sam.

The blast of the double-barrel startled Sam. Doe and The General appeared behind the bandit and she shot him in the back. His arms flew skyward, and the horse, no doubt hit by the pellets, left the country trying to buck his saddle to the sun. Seeing all this, the second masked man threw his hands up in surrender.

The stage driver and guard — now having recovered their weapons — came running to assist.

The guard shook his head. "We're damn lucky you two rode up when you did. We thought we were done for."

His partner nodded. "You can say that again, Jim."

The dead outlaw had cut holes in a flour sack and used it to hide his face. The driver kneeled down in the dust beside the desperado and pulled the crude mask off, revealing an ugly, tow-headed brute . . .

. . . with a wicked-looking scar over one eye.

Breathing heavily, Sam reined the mare to a halt.

How in the name of holy hell . . . ?

Wide-eyed, he slid off his mount and hobbled over to study the dead man's face.

Could it really be . . . ?

The driver whistled. "This guy was ugly enough as it is, but get a load of that scar over his eye. Must have been in a helluva fight somewhere."

"By God, yes he was," Sam whispered.

The dusty little man looked up at him. "You know this guy, mister?"

"You could say that."

Doe booted her shotgun, dismounted from The General, and walked over beside him. "This is man who kill his family."

"No foolin'?"

"No."

Searching the dead man's pockets, the driver produced a gold locket. Holding it up to the light, he checked both sides, then carefully opened it. "Strange thing for an outlaw to carry with him, huh?"

Leaning against the mare, Sam thought he was going to be sick. Clutching his stomach, he managed to hold out one gloved hand. "Let me have the locket. It belonged to some folks I once knew."

"Golly! Sure, mister." The driver stood up and handed over the shining gold oval and thin, matching chain. "How'd you come to know him?"

"Zane, clean the danged cotton out of your ears." The guard, still covering the other robber with his own scattergun, snorted. "This here's Sam Brennen, the bounty hunter. And that's his partner, Doe Mockingbird. We read about them in the newspaper a few days back."

"I'll be damned." The other would-be robber gave a mirthless little chuckle. "Cal was talking about you just yesterday. Said he

211

was going to find you and kill you. And your new woman."

The stage driver's eyes got wide. "Well, my God! Excuse me, sir. I didn't recognize you! Why, I read all about the Mulvain gang and all that stuff. We sure were lucky to have you all run onto us. Wow, if that isn't a co-incidence, I don't know what is."

Clutching the locket in his hand, Sam nodded weakly. "Like I said, we're just glad we could help."

"You okay, Mister Brennan?"

The throbbing in his leg was coming back. "My leg's a little messed up, that's all. My mare and I had a little disagreement with a bull a while back. You boys think you can deliver these two to the law in Globe?"

Jim — the guard — gave him a nod. "Be happy to. We'll get you the reward on 'em, too, Mister Brennan."

"Thanks." Sam turned back toward the horse and grasped the saddlehorn.

"You're welcome to ride in the coach."

"No, no. I'll be okay. Thanks." Painfully, he pulled himself up into the saddle. "We'll meet you in town. Let's go, Doe."

They rode in silence side-by-side on the road toward town. Sam held the locket in his free hand, turning it over and over again. His eyes were wet, and he kept wiping his nose on the sleeve of his shirt. Doe said nothing, merely keeping the mule abreast of the mare so he knew she was here with him. It had taken her a while to learn, but she'd come to understand that Sam was a man who would speak in his own time and not before.

The problem was that Sam didn't have the words to say anything just then. The evil men that had shattered his life and destroyed his dreams were no more — dead and sentenced to the flaming burning hell they surely deserved.

In spite of the evil done upon him, he'd somehow built a new life, conjured new dreams, without even realizing that's what he was doing. And yet it all had been driven by the need to avenge himself upon these monsters.

So where did that leave him now?

The cold winds whipped past them. When at last he spoke, his voice was dry as the desert around them.

"So he's dead." He looked out to the horizon. "It's over."

"Do you not feel better?"

He shook his head but remained silent.

Doe did not bother him again.

The stage had long passed them on the road, so word of their heroic deed was out before they reached Globe, and a crowd had gathered. Miners, cowboys, town folk, all standing in the street cheering as Sam and Doe rode in. A reporter broke out of the throng and waved his notebook at them.

"Did you know the dead robber, Mister Brennen?"

"Calvin Denton. He was wanted in Colorado for murder and rape." It was the first time he'd said it out loud. Until that moment, it hadn't yet been fully real.

Breathing deeply, he reined in the mare and looked to Doe.

"Yes." She nodded under her hat, looking grim. "It was him."

"Do you want to go on ahead to Bill's house? I know you dislike crowds."

"Only if you do not need me."

He gave her a wan smile. "Go ahead. I'll be along. I think these people have some more questions."

Tight-lipped, she gave him another quick nod, then spurred The General forward through the cheering, babbling crush of people. Sam watched her until she cleared the crowd and turned the far corner.

"Is it true that Miss Mockingbird really shot the bandit?" someone asked.

"Yes, it is. One hell of a shot, too, if I say so myself."

A large man in a brown suit pushed toward him. "Mister Brennen, I'm the town Marshal here. Blackwell Townsend. My friends call me Blacky. The Sheriff is gone right now, so I'll be the one taking care of the particulars with the stage incident. I'd like to shake your hand."

Sam took the offered hand. "Pleasure is mine."

"We'd like to buy you a drink."

"Well, boys, I'd consider that an honor, but someone will have to help me down. This left leg of mine is a little messed up."

"You bet." Several men rushed forward to assist. They literally carried him inside the warm bar. He described the entire incident to the eager audience crowded inside the *cantina,* the leg stretched across to another chair, as they drank beer with him. He told it straight, without any embellishments. After a while, Zane and Jim — the stage-coach driver and guard — arrived, so the story got told again, this time with their own spin placed upon it.

"By God we were lucky today!" Zane laughed and downed a shot of whiskey. "Sam and Doe rode in guns blazing, I tell you. Cut down that sumbitch Denton in a hail of lead."

Sam hesitated as he started to sip another

215

the beer. That sick feeling had hit him again. Why wasn't he more excited? Denton's death had proved to be little more than just another moment. The victory wasn't hollow — not with all these people around — but it had delivered no great relief. There was nothing in this musty-smelling saloon to illuminate his insides. There was far more meaning to him in the Christmas tree standing in the great room back at the ranch.

Finally, as the crowd began to thin, Sam stood and said his goodbyes. Blacky helped him out to the mare. The leg was hurting him worse than ever, buckling when he barely put any weight on it.

Black shook his head again. "Sam Brennen, I've never liked bounty hunters, but this county owes you a debt of gratitude."

"No, Blacky. We were just there, and we really like this country."

"Well, we owe you and that Indian gal."

Sam smiled politely and swung heavily, dragging the fringed chaps over the mare's rump as he mounted from the off side. With one final wave, he rode off toward the Johnson house.

Bill met him at the gate. "Sam, you've been on that leg too much."

"I'm okay."

Doe appeared in the door and helped him up the steps. "Missus Madera has sent for the doctor. She's worried we didn't do the right thing for it to begin with."

"I just need some rest." Sam waved them away, but then the leg buckled and he fell, nearly taking Doe with him.

"Come on, Doe, let's get him into bed." Bill grabbed his arm and helped him up. He took one side and she took the other.

"He left his crutches at home," Doe said. "But I think we will need some."

"Now, gal." Sam laughed as he pivoted on his good leg and swung into a large chair in the parlor.

Bill pulled a chair in from the kitchen and sat down in front of him.

"Sam, I think the little matter we spoke about earlier this month can be done now. You've become some kind of a folk hero now."

"Great!" Sam laughed and wiped the sweat from his brow. "Here I am all crippled up, and you can arrange for me to hobble up the aisle."

"Jose's gone after some crutches, and I think Juanita can go get the *padre* later on. The clerk owes me a favor, so I can get a license."

"Damn, Bill, where's your shotgun? Do

you know something I don't?"

"I just know you're anxious to get the deed done."

"That I am." He sighed. "I just wish I was in better shape. I feel a bit out of sorts at the moment."

"You look like it now, too." The banker grinned.

"Thanks." This brought on another round of laughter. This one went on so long Doe and Juanita finally came in to see what was going on.

Finally, the doorbell rang. Bill rose to answer it, leaving Sam in the capable hands of Doe and Mrs. Madera. He appeared again a few minutes later with the doctor in tow.

Doc Watson was a frowning, eye-glassed, short, fat man who punched and tapped on the bad leg until Sam was sure he had to be rebreaking the damn thing.

"It will heal if you stay off the damn thing." He cussed gruffly, pulling off gold-rimmed glasses and cleaning them with a white kerchief. Shaking his head, he took a bottle of laudanum out of his bag. "Pain gets bad, take a tablespoon of this."

"Was it broke?"

"Bruised, cracked, broke. Can't see inside that skin, but sometimes bruises heal slower

218

than bones."

"How much do I owe you?"

"Two dollars. Can't say I did do much for you."

"Satisfied my mind." Sam dug into his pocket and pulled out the money.

"If you just stay off the damn thing for a week more — it should be two or three, but you won't! — it will feel better."

"Yeah, yeah. I'll try."

"Do more than try, young man. Or we'll be seeing one another sooner than you'd like." With that, the doctor grabbed his bag and left.

Bill saw him out, then returned.

"Well, that settles it. You two are staying here until the leg gets better."

The leg improved slowly. By week's end, Sam could walk on it again. The Sheriff, a balding, heavyset man of about fifty, came by to pay his respects after the stagecoach caper.

He seemed particularly curious about the other prisoner's story.

"This Bobby Wilks character said he joined Denton over in New Mexico, and that Denton seemed to be trailing you. Did he have some kind of a grudge against you?"

Sam sighed and shook his head. "Denton

murdered my wife and stepdaughters last year up in Colorado. Other than that, I can't tell you much of anything about him."

"Wilks seems to think you'd busted his head up in Wichita. . . ."

"You know how that goes. I don't remember him. I've searched my mind. Maybe Wyatt or one of the others did it, but I've had a long time to think about it and haven't come up with anything"

"Never you mind. He's dead and you're alive, and that's all that matters now. The stage line is going to send you a hundred-dollar reward."

"Fine. Maybe we can find some orphans that need it?"

"Your money." The lawman shrugged.

"They don't have to know."

"I can handle that."

Bill saw the lawman to the door. Finally alone again, Sam sagged back into his chair and searched his memories of Wichita once again. For the life of him, he couldn't recall ever having an issue with the likes of Cal Denton. With a mug like that sumbitch had, he should easily remember if they'd ever gotten tangled up. Bur there was nothing there.

Frustrated, he gave up and turned his attention to other matters.

Bill had given him an update on the sawmill operation that morning. Things were going well, and the mill had just signed a contract to supply a mining company that would turn an almost immediate profit. He'd also heard from Thompson, his agent in Prescott. The gold mine deal had been signed, sealed, and delivered, and the first payment wired into Sam's account here in Globe.

Combined with the improvements being made down on the ranch, business matters were all on the up and up.

And yet Sam still felt restless.

Maybe that was because he still had one old debt left to pay.

"Hey, Bill. What's the word on getting me the location of the Peraltas?"

His friend frowned. "You're in no condition to be going after those two bandits, Sam."

"I know that, damn it. Just tell me what's going on."

Bill sighed. "I had word earlier this week that the Peraltas are moving some stolen cattle down to the border."

"Why in the Sam Hill hadn't you told me?"

"Like I said, you're in no condition to ride at the moment, let alone track down a gang

221

of ruthless thieves and murderers. I know you, and I know how you work. You'd be up and out that door two minutes after I'd told you. What kind of friend would I be to you — let alone Doe — if I you do that?"

"Damn it, still. . . ." Sam hung his head. Infuriating as it was, there was no arguing Bill's reasoning. "How come no one else rounds them up? There's wanted posters out on them everywhere."

The banker shrugged. "They're mean and keep on the move. You ought to take some gunmen with you when you head out to tangle with them."

"We'll see when this leg gets better."

The priest dropped by later that afternoon to explain that he would be pleased to marry Sam and Doe. Since Sam was not baptized in the church, though, they must be married in front of the rail.

Sam looked over at Doe, who simply shook her head. The message was clear — it didn't matter. The marriage was the important thing.

"Then it's all set, I guess." He put out his hand and the priest shook it. "We will come to your church and be married next Tuesday evening."

"*Señor,* it is very unusual, but I think it is what God would will."

"*Padre,* we are pleased that you will marry us."

"God be with you." The priest made the sign of the cross and hurried out.

Standing beside his chair, Doe leaned down and hugged him. There was a spring in her step as she headed out of the room for some coffee. Sam thought she might be ready to do a dance in her boots. Then again, he decided, it was well past time to be getting this done.

"Doe Mockingbird will soon be just Doe Brennen," she teased as she came back in with the coffee.

"In Missouri, most folks have two names like Frank John or Betty Jo. So, I guess you'll be Doe Mockingbird Brennen."

"Brennan part is the important one." She smiled and left him to his coffee.

The wedding was very formal. Juanita had spared no expense planning it. She ordered Doe a custom-made white lace dress from a seamstress in Phoenix and a fancy new suit for Sam. She ordered flowers, too, apparently by the bushel. The church was decked out with so many floral arrangements, you could smell them all from the street.

Inside, the church was lit by candles and the last rays of the setting sun. All in white,

Doe waited for him at the low rail separating the nave and the altar, a sheer veil pulled down over her face. Sweating in his suit, Sam limped slowly down the aisle toward her.

The priest spoke solemnly about the bonds of matrimony, of their vows to one another and the responsibilities. When it came time for them to repeat the vows and say their "I dos," their voices were so soft, neither Juanita — standing beside Doe — nor Bill — standing beside Sam — could hear more than a whisper.

Finally, the priest raised his hands and made the sign of the cross.

"I pronounce you man and wife. You may kiss the bride."

Sam swallowed the lump in his throat. Everything else had faded except for Doe. They were alone in the great church as surely as they had ever been on the plains, in the camp, or the great featherbed at the *hacienda*. As gently as he could, he grasped the edges of Doe's veil and pulled it up and over her head. Her eyes were bright in the light of the candles, her smile radiant. It was the greatest joy of his life to bend his face to hers in that moment and kiss her on the lips.

Their union had finally been sealed.

Now officially married, they turned to their two friends and joined them in celebration.

Doe hugged Jaunita tightly. "I am so very happy. You are very good to an Apache girl."

Juanita wiped tears from her eyes. "Oh, Doe, that's silly. You're a woman, greater than most I've known."

Bill gave Sam a hug, then gave him a friendly punch on the arm. "Where will you go on your honeymoon?"

"Out to the ranch. We need to check on Miguel. Sleep in our own bed."

"Tonight, you'll sleep in the same bed at my house." Bill waggled his brows suggestively. "Tomorrow you can go back to the ranch."

"By the time we're done, I'll owe you a hotel bill that'll break the bank."

"It's a good thing I own that bank, huh?" They laughed. "Hey, we love the company. Besides, you'll both need to come back in April when Juanita and I will get married."

"Wonderful!" He pumped the banker's hand with joy. Then he grabbed Juanita by the waist and swung her as best he could with his sore leg. Her eyes were as happy as Sam's when he put her down.

"Calm down!" Doe slapped him on the shoulder. "We are still in the church, Sam

Brennen."

"Yes, Missus Brennen. Why don't we go home and celebrate?"

They were all gathered at the Johnsons' table when the bell rang. Bill excused himself and put his napkin down to see who was there. He returned with a leather-dressed *vaquero* holding a huge *sombrero* in his hands.

"Sorry for the interruption, folks. Sam, this man has word of the Peralta brothers. You need to know that they're in jail down in Sonora, and he expects them to be loose in a few days."

The other man nodded. "*Señor,* they have friends in high places. They will be out very soon."

"How soon?"

"I do not know, but it took me three days to ride here with the news so. . . ." The *vaquero* shrugged. "My poor horse is nearly dead. I only hope I came in time."

Bill shook his head. "You will be paid well, and the horse can be replaced. Get a room tonight and come to the bank tomorrow."

"*Señor,* these men are the worst kind of outlaws."

"We know."

The man left, and the foursome sat quietly. It was almost time to send the newlyweds off to bed, but there was one last toast to be made.

Bill raised his glass. "To the bride and groom. May their first night together be happy . . . and fruitful."

"Bill!" Doe nearly spit out her wine.

The banker laughed and winked at Juanita, who blushed.

"Here it is, for real this time." He raised the glass one more time. "To long life and friendship."

"To long life and friendship," they all echoed.

"Thank you, Bill." After finishing his own glass, Sam stood. "Well, I think it's time for bed. Can you do me a favor in the morning, though, Bill?"

"Name it."

"I want to send word to Miguel that I'll be delayed a few days in getting out to the ranch."

Doe eyed him from across the table. "Why?"

"You know why. You can stay here."

"Sam Brennen, I will be going to Sonora, too."

"Doe . . ."

"I am not just the horse tender now."

This made him snort. "Like that ever stopped you."

Doe stood and pushed her chair up to the table. "Come. Let us go argue in bedroom, so we do not embarrass our friends."

In the room, Sam sat on the edge of the bed. He toed his boot off and looked at the floor.

For Doe's part, she continued to pace the floor. "There are more important things for us than those bad men."

He nodded and studied the boots.

"What if I am unable to have children?"

"Doe, my Lord! Why are we on *that* subject?"

"The woman you married may never have a baby!"

"Fine, whatever. That doesn't worry me. Tomorrow, we ride to Sonora. I need someone to back me up." He rocked her slender form in his arms.

"You are right." She unhooked the white wedding dress and let it fall to the floor.

Sam shook his head at the sight of her and remembered their first night on the prairie in Colorado.

CHAPTER No. 16

The buckboard was light, and with the two good bays, Sam intended to catch the stage from Casa Grande to Tucson. The horses were hot-blooded and capable of covering lots of country. Sam reined them around the curves, causing the wheels to slide.

Doe grasped the iron rail on the seat and leaned into Sam as he charged the horses on. The ride proved bumpy, and they laughed as the front wheel struck a rock and nearly unseated both of them.

In Casa Grande, they climbed on the stage and headed for Tucson. Stopping at the stage station at Picacho, Sam stretched his legs. The sore one was aching, but he tried to hide it. Fat chance of that, though.

"Your leg is not well, is it?"

"A little sore."

"We better get on the stage." By the early light of dawn, they were approaching Tucson, sleepy-eyed from just a few hours of napping.

Sam swung down heavily and went into the stage office to check on the next stage south.

"Yes, sir, we'll be going to Nogales in about ten minutes."

Sam paid him for two tickets and went outside for some fresh air. Doe handed him a burrito from a nearby street vendor. They stood waiting as the coach pulled up, and the driver nodded for them to get in.

Climbing in the coach, Doe sat against the right window and Sam on the left. Reaching out, they held hands as the car ran south at full speed.

"Doe, we're going into another world down in Mexico. The law is . . . well, different there."

"These are still white people?"

"The Apaches are different than the Hopi?"

"Okay. You win. What should we expect of Mexican law?"

"That's my girl." Sam laughed over the racket of the rattling coach, hoofbeats, and the urging of the driver. "The Peraltas have friends in Mexico, so we must be careful. Or we'll be the ones in some cockroach-infested jail."

"You have plan?" She leaned over on his

shoulder, only to be bolted up by a jolt of the coach.

"Stagecoaches are poor places to be romantic." He grinned at her. "No plan, my love. We're just going to Mexico."

"You will think of what to do."

The sun sat low in the January sky when the stage halted in the small border post of Nogales.

Dismounting, Sam helped her out of the coach and searched about. Entering the stage line office, he saw the attendant busy stuffing the mail sack.

"Hotel?"

"The best is across the border, the San Marcos."

"Thanks." Sam tipped his hat and guided Doe out in front of him.

A very sleepy horse hitched to a rather rickety carriage sat out front. The driver rushed up to them and bowed graciously.

"We need a ride over to the San Marcos."

"*Sí, Señor,* the San Marcos is a grand place to stay."

"Fine, let's get going." Sam held his hand out and helped Doe up into the carriage compartment.

"*Sí, vamos caballo!*"

The sleepy horse responded with a start

that resembled a harness race. Rushing past the border guardhouse with a wave by the driver, they swept into Mexico, coming to a screeching halt before the hotel. "Fast enough, *Señor*?"

"Plenty!"

"*Señor,* do you perhaps need a guide tomorrow?"

"Perhaps. Be here at 7:30 in the morning."

"I will be here at 7:00 waiting for you."

Sam nodded, paid the man, and oversaw the porter getting their bags.

The next morning the cab man was waiting in anticipation when they came out of the hotel.

"First, I need some information. Are the Peralta brothers still in jail here?"

"The Peralta brothers? Oh, yes, you may be in time."

"Time? For what?"

"Are they your friends?"

"Not really. Why?"

"We better hurry, because they are going to shoot them in a little while."

"*Shoot* them?"

"*Sí, Señor,* they were found guilty of murdering a very rich man and raping his daughter."

232

Sam looked over at Doe. "We are not in a hurry."

"Oh, but you will miss the firing squad. Everyone in Nogales is there."

The coach arrived in record time. The two men in white linen prison uniforms stood before an adobe wall, facing the big crowd.

Sam helped Doe out of the coach in no hurry. The crowd was yelling insults at the convicted killers in Spanish.

Defiantly, the pair curled their lips at the crowd. The guard stuck a cigar in each mouth as their last request and lit them. Blowing smoke out their noses, the Peraltas seemed to enjoy the attention in a surly way.

Doe narrowed her eyes. "It is them."

"Justice will be served, then."

Just as he'd said it, though, there came the sound of charging horses and gunshots. Sam swept Doe up and into a doorway. Drawing his Colt, he stood in front of her as the screaming crowd parted, and the outlaws' compadres came to the rescue.

A band of six horsemen rode into view, well-armed and leading two spare horses. One of the guards was shot and fell dead. The mustached Peralta, now somehow loose, grabbed the dead man's gun and waved it at the crowd, laughing.

Another guard, shot down, pitched forward. The Peraltas mounted the horses the rescuers had brought.

Sam was holding his place in front of Doe, who he had to force into crouch. In a clatter of hooves, the band of outlaws were gone, with only a few parting shots to hurry them on their way.

Sam held his fire. It was useless, and no more defensible than the doorway was, there was no need to draw return fire.

"Why do I not have my gun?" She gave an angry shake of her head.

Sam holstered the Colt and pulled her up by the arm, gently. "So you can live to get those bastards."

There was much commotion. The officer in charge was sending his men in all directions to get their horses. Leaving Doe on the sidewalk, Sam stepped into the street and walked over to the officer.

"Señor?"

"What do you want, *gringo?* I saw you in the crowd. Why did you not shoot those *banditos?*"

"I only had one gun and there were too many of them. You tell me, though. . . . How the hell did their hands get untied?"

The officer waved impatiently. "Nevermind. What do you want?"

Nevermind. Sam bit his tongue. "Where

234

will they go now? The Peraltas?"

"Across the border, I would assume. Since there is a price on their heads here in Mexico."

"How much?"

"One thousand *pesos* now."

"For one or both?"

"Apiece, and I assure you, *Señor,* the authorities may double that amount." Another policeman walked up, leading the officer's horse. "Now, if you don't have any more questions, I must mount a pursuit."

Sam was sure the "pursuit" this man would mount would be come to nothing, but decided not to say anything. He simply nodded and let the man ride off.

The cab man appeared unharmed and more than slightly puzzled about Sam's conversation with the officer. He was so pleased to see his meal ticket unharmed, however, he actually looked relieved.

Sam leaned forward and spoke to the man. "I want three good horses and an Indian tracker. Do you know a good one?"

The man nodded and whipped the thin horse into a run.

Doe stole a glance at Sam as she climbed back into the coach.

Sam dropped into his seat and wiped his brow. "We'll get them."

The stable of his driver's choice sat in disrepair. The owner looked like he had eaten too many *frijoles*. Once he showed Sam his corral of horses, though, Sam changed his mind about the man. All of the mounts were prime and well broke. Sam rode the ones he thought suited him, then chose a pair of saddles and a crossbuck pack saddle.

After thirty minutes dickering, the portly stable man decided that he had reached the best deal he could make. They shook hands and Sam handed over the agreed-upon amount.

As Doe saddled their new purchases, Sam turned to the cab man and asked about the tracker he had in mind.

"He is a very good tracker. He can trail a mouse over a stone wall."

"Does he have a horse?"

"*No, Señor,* he is a Yacqui. They do not need horses."

"Go find him and bring him to the hotel. The *Federales* aren't too anxious to chase down the Peraltas, and they have a good start. We're in the President's suite."

"*Sí,* I will be back to your hotel in one hour."

Sam relayed this to Doe. "One hour and we'll have our tracker."

236

"I can read tracks." She sounded impatient, and more than just a little put-out.

"You don't know the country, love. This tracker should. That may save our lives, and I aim to take mighty good care of your life."

She only nodded at this. "I need my shotgun."

"It's in the suitcase at the hotel. I'm going after some supplies, so when our tracker gets here, we can leave. Here's the money to pay for our room and meals. I'll be back."

"Me, pay for the room?"

"You are Missus Sam Brennen now, aren't you?"

Doe smiled, then ducked her head as if she was about to be hit.

Climbing up on the bay horse, she rode back toward the San Marcos, passing ox carts and burro trains on the streets. She was steeling herself to the task ahead. Sam Brennen sometimes was a hard man for an Indian girl to figure out. With him, she must be ready to swallow the whole world he lived in. *It's easy, just act like you own it, and they will never know the difference.* That is what he would say. But *this* Indian would never own a hotel — too many stinking pots to empty.

"Mister Brennen and I will be checking out," she told the clerk, her head held high.

"Oh, I thought you might stay another night?"

Doe's heart was pounding in her throat. "No. Please prepare the, ah, bill. And I would appreciate help with the bags. I shall be right down."

"Of course, Missus Brennen. We will have someone up to help get your bags immediately."

With a swirl of her skirt, Doe started up the steps with her head so high she was afraid she might fall over backwards. Swearing to herself as she climbed the stairs, she nearly tripped. It so upset her, she ducked her head down to search around the staircase, hoping no one saw her miss. Crazy times — and the Peralta brothers were getting farther way.

Finishing her business, she waited in front of the hotel where her horse was hitched with the suitcases. The wait seemed like an eternity, but before long Sam rode up the narrow street leading the pack horse.

He winked at he as he dismounted. "Seen our wild cart-jockey yet?"

"No."

"Did you get the bill all paid?"

"Of course." Doe flung her shoulders back and raised her chin. "Am I Missus Sam

238

Brennan now or not?"

Sam laughed. "No doubt about it."

The cab driver showed up about ten minutes later. He arrived wild-eyed and out of breath, with a tiny Indian in the back of the carriage. Stepping down from his bench, he opened the door and doffed his hat with a flourish.

"*Señor,* may I present Jose Vasquez. The best tracker in all of Arizona, Sonora, or Chihuahua."

Sam sized the little man up. "Jose, is it true that you don't need a horse?"

Vasquez shook his head.

"Did your friend tell you we wanted to track down the Peraltas?"

"Cost one dollar ever' day." His voice was very soft, almost a whisper.

"Price is fine, let's go."

The Yauqui stepped over and fell in beside their horses with a step that spoke of his ability to keep up with them.

Sam dug out some coins for the driver and they shook hands. The guide spent much energy hollering after his customers about wanting to work again with such generous Americanos.

Sam tossed the lead rope to Doe. She grinned as she caught it and followed

239

behind. She almost startled when the man spoke to her in Apache. "Are you with the white-eye?"

"Yes, he is my husband," she replied in the same tongue. "Do not try to betray him. He will kill you. Or I will."

"I simply wondered why you rode with him. I will earn my dollar."

"Remember to." Sam who had turned to listen in and gave her a curious glance. She grinned. "Jose did not understand that I am Missus Sam Brennen."

He laughed. "Did you tell him he couldn't have you?"

"Of course."

"Jose, where do you figure the Peraltas have gone?"

"The *Federales* pursued them for only a few minutes. If they were in Mexico, they would still be after them."

Sam waved his hat off toward the horizon. "Lead the way, we'll try to keep up."

The tracker set off ahead of them and seemed oblivious to the activity he jogged through. Sam reined around the freight wagons, and Doe followed with her pack animal.

With the little Indian in the lead, they crossed over to the American side of the border with nothing more than a nod from the border guards. Avoiding people on foot in the road, they climbed the hill on the Tucson road.

Finally, the tracker stopped. "I must go east and find the trail. It is not here on the road. There is a watering place at those mountains." He pointed to the northeast. "It is easy to find. I will meet you there on the west side at sundown."

"Be careful, Jose. These guys are tough."

"Sí, Señor." He took off running through the mesquite and cat claw in his high-top moccasins, leaving Sam to shake his head in wonder.

Sam and Doe struck out on the cattle trails that wound through the tall desert scrub. Scaring up a few grazing cows and their bald-faced calves, he admired the offspring of the longhorn cows.

Climbing a long ridge, they rode it eastward, staying to the skyline. By noon, Sam decided, as broken as this country was, it would take most of the day finding their way to the base of the purple mountain Jose had chosen. The spiny barrel cactus studded the hillsides along with the more luxuriant greasewood.

There was little sign of man as they rode on, spotting an occasional cow with a brand unfamiliar to Sam. Some hard-pressed mustangs fled down the sandy dry bottom racing from the unseen pursuers. In a moment, two boys came hard after them swinging ropes and screaming at their mounts to hurry. Sam saw one look back in apparent curiosity before he turned, intent on the mustangs.

"They're having a good time." Sam was almost envious.

"Wonder if they ever chased burros?"

"Bet they'd be good at it." He smiled, giving his horse the lead and moving out.

They were approaching some cottonwood trees that had to signify a watering place at the base of the mountain. The sun was getting low, and the air was cooling as the day lost its heat. A large waterhole seemed serene enough except for some cattle lounging around chewing their cud, an obvious reference to the absence of humans. Sensing their approach, the wary range animals moved off into the brushy surroundings.

"Keep them on your mind," Sam warned. Dismounting, his leg barely held him as he stood holding the horn. The bay horse blew wearily, then he shook the empty saddle.

"Does your leg hurt, Sam Brennen?"

"Yes, Missus Doe." He slipped the rawhide lace off the hammer on his Colt. "Jose, that you?"

"Sí, Señor." The tracker stepped out from behind a large, gnarled trunked cottonwood.

Doe looked mildly at the two and shook her head in disbelief. "How did you know he was there? I did not see him."

He grinned. "I sensed something was there. Birds or something."

"Ask him how he knows Apache."

"Jose?"

"I have lived among your people, and I know that your name was Star of Morning when you lived among them, too. I also know that your brother is at San Carlos and mourns your death."

"Did this Yacqui say my brother is on a reservation?"

Sam put out his arms. "Easy, Doe."

"He is there as the great chief. There are people there you would know."

"Liar!"

"Doe! This man has no reason to lie. Is that your Apache name?"

"Yes, but my brother is a warrior." She broke down and fell to her knees.

Sam swung the bad leg out and held her shoulder. "It may not be as bad you see it."

Jose bowed before her. "I thought that you would be glad to hear of him."

"I am sorry. You bring good news." She

tried to restore her composure by pushing out her chest and raising her chin in defiance. Then she spun on her heel and made herself busy setting up camp.

Blowing out a breath, Sam hobbled over to a nearby log and sat heavily. "Have you found sign of the Peraltas?" he asked.

Jose nodded. "They are at a ranch of a poor man not half a day from this place. There are signs of them in the camp. Those *pistoleros* . . . they are very mean *hombres, Señor.*"

"Can the camp be taken?"

"I think so, but we will have to be careful."

"I do not ask you to fight our battle." He rubbed his whisker-bristled face.

"These men have scalped my people and the Apache. They are dogs that need to be killed. I wish to help you get them."

"We will see what Doe has to say about that."

She did not look up from her work. "He will be a good fighter."

Sam nodded. Well, that was settled at least.

He turned back to the Yacqui. "Jose, make us a plan in the dirt of how this place is."

The man took his time in the dimming light, drawing the ranch house and corrals, showing Sam the cover that might hide them.

"Are you afraid of the night?" Sam asked the Indian as they ate the warm bread she had made and sipped the coffee.

"It would be better, but your leg is going to slow you down."

"I'll be there." Sam blew impatiently at the steaming coffee.

"He is a very stubborn man, but he shoots straight." Doe squatted beside her fire. After her meal, they slept a few hours and were ready to move on with the moon to guide them.

CHAPTER No. 17

They left the pack horse, and Sam somehow managed to get back up on his own horse. The little sleep he'd gotten on the ground had not helped his throbbing leg one bit.

The Yacqui led the way in the silver light of the rising moon. Sam followed along behind, with Doe bringing up the rear. A coyote howled to its mate on the mountain above them, and a desert owl hooted. Doe answered it, and the night bird answered back.

"You are so good you fool the wise one," the tracker said over his shoulder as they slipped through the brush.

"I learned from my people."

Leaving the horses, they approached the little ranch from the east. The going was difficult for Sam with his bad leg, but he limped on without complaint. Soon enough, they gathered on a small ridge just above the darkened adobe house where the Peraltas had holed up. There was not a sound except the shuffling of the outlaws' horses in the corral.

Jose whispered, "There is a single guard down by the horses — he is sitting or sleeping. I will take him out. Three hoots, and we can begin to take them."

Sam nodded, then watched the little Yacqui slip silently down the slope. If one did not know he was there, they could not see the quiet stealth of the man as he moved off the steep hillside.

Doe started slowly that way, as silent in her boots as the gentle breezes fluttering the cottonwood leaves. Bent low with the shotgun in her hand, she moved opposite Sam's position. The faint trace of dawn streaked the eastern sky as Sam began his own slow, painful descent down the rocky slope with the repeating rifle.

This whole deal was plumb damn crazy. One Yacqui armed with Joe Sunday's pistol and a knife, one Indian woman with a double-barrel and a coat pocket full of 12-gauge buckshot, and a cripple with a Winchester and a Colt. Against two of the most ruthless killers to roam the desert borderlands and God knew how many *pistoleros* riding with them.

Still thirty feet to go to get behind the

adobe wall. Sam was breathing hard, the pain in his leg making him wince as he edged toward the pile of adobe bricks. The scraping of his boots was deafening in his own ears as he half-crawled into position.

An owl hooted — Jose was ready to go.

Sam cocked the loaded Winchester. On the porch ahead of him, one of the outlaws was sacked out in a wooden chair by the front door and side window. With any luck, the rest of the crew would be asleep inside.

He took a deep breath. "This is the law! Squaw killers and murderers, throw out your guns and come out with your hands up!"

On the far side of the house, Doe leveled her shotgun and pulled the trigger, blowing out one of the windows and spraying buckshot indiscriminately over the shocked, cursing, sleepy outlaws within. Down by the corral, Jose aimed a shot from the pistol at the front door, and Sam followed it up with some lead from the Winchester aimed at the front door.

"How the hell many's out there?"

The dark figure of a man came bursting out the front door. Jose took careful aim and dropped him backwards as the outlaw's pistol discharged into the thatched roof of the porch.

Sam had been ready with the rifle. He swung it to the window and snapped off a shot at the head behind a pistol that peeked out. Flying splinters blinded the would-be shooter as he fell back screaming.

Doe let off another deadly blast of the scattergun into the window, followed by screams of protest from inside. A quick *click* signaled that she had reloaded, and the commotion inside told Sam more of the outlaws were fixing to bust out.

"We've got you covered. Put those guns down and come out, hands high."

The answer, as expected, was a round of wild shooting as the *banditos* made a brazen rush for freedom. Jose, though, was very deliberate and cut down the first outlaw from his position beside the corral. Doe's shotgun sent another to the ground screaming with his leg shot. Another took one of Sam's .44/40 slugs in his shoulder that sent him sprawling inside.

"How many are out there?" a voice in the house demanded.

"Pedro's shot in the shoulder and Renaldo is out there dead."

"What do you expect?"

Sam saw the flicker of fire, and he knew what Jose had done. He had twisted hay around a rock. Igniting it, he had thrown the flaming object on the roof of the thatched porch with accuracy. The dry palm fronds instantly began to flame where it had landed.

Charge Number Two came on. The battered outlaws charged out shooting in desperation. Sam's rifle dropped the first one. Then he saw them throw down their arms as someone slipped out the window.

Rolling back on his left side painfully, Sam drew his Colt and aimed it at the escaping outlaw. The flaming pistol of the escapee blasted at him as Sam dropped down. His bullets whizzed overhead and hit the adobe pile with a thud that told Sam they were close.

Rising up, he could see a pistol aimed at his face not ten feet away. He was staring down death in the long barrel if the evil face behind it was accurate. His time had come, here on the ground unable to even twist back for cover. The shot was deafening. He closed his eyes to await the inevitable, the reaper was coming.

All the good and bad he'd ever done was going to be climaxed behind an adobe wall on a poor desert ranch by nothing but a worthless bunch of scum. If Doe and Jose succeeded, they'd probably always count him as their best friend. But the shot he thought was intended for him instead had silenced the attacker.

The outlaws surrendered. In terrible pain, Sam used the rifle for a crutch to get up. After a quick and painful moment, Doe was under his arm.

"They have given up."

He coughed. "Why not, half of them's dead."

Jose was busy disarming them. The healthy gang members were tied up and seated on the ground. The shot-up outlaws cried and moaned, lying on the ground. None of them were drawing any sympathy, though. One of the brothers had a minor wound, probably from Doe's buckshot.

They'd live to hang, Sam figured. He directed Jose to go find help. If they were lucky, they could have the law here by noon. Meanwhile, he and Doe would sit and be on guard.

Three days later, they stood waiting for the driver to load the stagecoach in front of the Nogales office. The Santa Cruz County Sheriff and the lieutenant from the Mexican *Federales* shook his hand to thank them for bringing in the brothers. They were locked up in an American jail.

"This land will be twice as good without that bunch," the Sheriff said.

"Well, we better load up. We've got a ranch to run up north." Sam gritted his teeth and followed Doe up aboard the coach.

Easing himself down, Sam grinned at Doe. Then he looked over at the stone-faced Jose who sat with arms folded. The scout had been invited to join them on the ranch since there was no work at the border for anyone.

"First stage ride?"

Jose nodded.

"It won't be smooth," Doe promised him with a smile.

The stage started north with a holler out of the driver, and they were off. Shaking his head, Sam closed his eyes. It was a long way from the first afternoon he set eyes on a bundle of hides in Colorado.

"Doe Brennen, we're going home."

"Yes, Sam Brennen. I am ready to see Miguel and the rest of our people." Her voice was full of pride.

He squeezed her shoulder, and the stage jolted, sending them both in the air nearly onto Jose. They all laughed as Sam commented about how rough stages were to ride.

They were going home.

■ ■ ■ ■

BOUNTY RIDERS

A TRIBUTE TO
DUSTY RICHARDS
BY J.B. HOGAN

■ ■ ■ ■

Shadows of fast-moving clouds, lit by the fading sun, sped across the nearby Cooper Mountains, stretched almost to the Stephens homestead. The blistering heat of day was giving way to the cooling, tranquilizing approach of dusk. Here in the Arizona portion of the New Mexico Territory in the early 1850s, the Stephens family — transplants from eastern Pennsylvania — eked out a living on sixty acres of scrub land that scarcely kept a handful of scrawny cattle and sheep alive.

Besides the rectangular white adobe Stephens home, there was little to indicate this was settled land, save a few scrawny chickens and some bony pigs that wandered about outside a poorly fenced in, barely surviving vegetable garden. It was a far more difficult life here in the desert southwest than the settlers had believed and hoped it would be when, just a few short years ago, they had chosen to seek their fortune in America's growing western lands.

Some quarter of a mile from the house, seventeen-year-old Zack Stephens, sweaty and dirty from a hard day's work, completed repairs on a break in a rail fence that, like everything about the Stephens place, just managed to serve its intended purpose. While Zack worked, his fifteen-year-old sister, Clara, approached from the house behind him, her figure growing larger over his left shoulder as she neared.

Clara carried a small pail of water and a dipper in one hand. Her other hand was held behind her back as if she were hiding something. Zack noticed Clara's presence when she was some yards away. He glanced over his shoulder but immediately turned back to work. Clara reached his side and waited, somewhat impatiently, for him to stop working and pay attention to her. She rattled the dipper in the pail and shifted back and forth from one foot to the other. Finally, Zack finished repairing a length of rail and turned toward his sister. She handed him the water with a sheepish grin. He drank warily, keeping an eye on her.

"What? What are you looking at me like that for?"

Zack replaced the dipper in the pail and

set it carefully on the dusty soil by his feet. He made sure the precious liquid was secure in the pail by lodging it between a fence post and the stock of a long, double barrel, 12-gauge shotgun with a "Z" carved on the stock.

"You have that look. What are you up to, now, sister?"

She shuffled back and forth, smiling shyly. Zack gave her a hard look, then shook his head and smiled. He signaled with his hand for her to show him what was behind her back. She pulled away and put both hands behind her back.

"Come on, Clara, what do you have there?"

He playfully tried to grab her hands. She managed to evade him again, and he turned back to his work. She quickly produced her hidden treasure, a chunk of coarse brown bread and a hard-boiled egg and held them out for Zack, but he was not looking at her.

"Here, I brought this for you."

Zack turned and eyed the food. "The others need it more than me, sister."

"No, they don't. You work as hard as Papa and don't eat half as much. You eat so little and work so hard, brother, please take it."

He looked at the coarse bread and plain, boiled egg, yet licked his lips as if they were a steak and baked potato. Clara handed him the bread and he took it, biting into it hungrily. She shelled the egg and handed it to him.

"Thank you."

"You're welcome."

While Zack munched on the food, Clara stood by watching him. He savored the last of the food, eating small bites that he chewed slowly and deliberately.

"This old desert is just so big, and empty, Zack." Clara pointed out across the land. "It's so lonely here. Wouldn't you like to be in a city, with stores and things to buy and people everywhere." Zack glanced past Clara but said nothing. "I want to go to California where there are cities and people — things to do. It's so . . . so dirty, and hot and empty here."

Zack hurriedly finished his food and stepped in front of Clara. Over her shoulder, he saw a small group of Indians on horseback, some riding double, coming up to the front of the Stephens home. He stiffened and put his arm on Clara's shoulder.

"I just hate it here, Zack, I've just got to . . . what?"

"Shh. Stop." He held up his hand.

"Zack, don't you shush me. You're not. . . ."

He grabbed her by the arm with one hand and put the index finger of his other hand against her lips.

"Look."

She turned and saw the arrival of the Indians at the house. Zack motioned for her to kneel down.

"Stay here."

He grabbed the shotgun and walked slowly toward the house. Clara followed him.

"Zack!" She hissed. "Don't leave me here, please."

They paused for a moment when their father emerged at the front of the house and gesticulated toward the Indians.

"Stay behind me."

They continued to walk carefully, slowly. As they walked, Zack broke down the shotgun to make sure it was loaded. He closed it back up as quietly as he could, but at least one Indian boy heard and looked over. From the distance that separated them, the Indian boy and Zack, for the briefest of seconds, sized each other up.

Abruptly, the Indians turned and began to ride away, though slowly. By the time Zack and Clara reached the house, they were well away. Their mother and little sister came out of the house to join their father.

"What did they want, Papa?" Clara asked breathlessly. "Who were they?"

"Did you know them, Pa?" Zack pointed his shotgun toward the receding figures of the Indians. "Were they hostiles?"

Mr. Stephens, a tall, lean man with a weather-beaten face, held up his hand to calm Clara and Zack.

"Everything is all right. You two settle down. Clara, come in and help your mother. Zack, better go to the creek, boy, and get us a couple of buckets of water. Your mother will be needing it for supper. Go on now."

"Yes, Sir."

When the women went back inside, taking the little girl with them, Mr. Stephens put his hand on Zack's shoulder.

"Boy, check the shed and the outhouse on your way. Don't want nobody hiding out there."

"Should I take the double barrel?"

"There won't be no need." Mr. Stephens took the shotgun. "Just check, it'll be all right."

"All right, Pa."

Zack walked around the house to the shed. He opened the door and grabbed a pair of water buckets. Then he did a quick check of the outhouse, and with another check all around the place, headed off to the creek.

Zack dipped one of two buckets into a not particularly deep part of the slow running, narrow creek below the Stephens home. An already full bucket sat on the bank. The creek, really more of a wash, was deep set between two sand banks about six feet high on either side. Down by the water, the Stephens house was out of sight.

It was nearing dusk now, and very still, and Zack took his time filling the second bucket. This was the pleasant, quiet part of the desert day and he drank in the cooling air, the flight of a cactus wren, the light sigh of wind on an ocotillo branch. Suddenly, he paused and turned his head toward the house. A door slammed and a cow lowed.

Zack grabbed the buckets and hurried up the bank. On high ground, in the fading light, he could see the house. There was a flurry of activity around it and audible cries.

He dropped the buckets and tore across the desert scrub toward the house, yelling at the top of his lungs.

"Indians! Pa, Momma. Get away from there. Clara, Janie, run. Run, everybody."

As he got within a hundred yards of the house, the first flares of a fire shot up inside the building. He stopped momentarily to grab a big slab from a pile of scrap wood, then hurried on. Just when he reached the house, three Indians appeared from around the side and he was instantly engaged in hand to hand battle.

The largest Indian was distinguished by a large scar on his left cheek. The younger boy whom Zack had seen before hung to the back. The third attacker had eyes dulled by a gray film that gave him a terrifying appearance. He led the attack against Zack.

Swinging his slab of wood wildly, Zack managed to hit Dull Eyes hard against one shoulder, dislocating it and causing the man to cry out. Before Zack could turn toward the other two, they both hit him solidly with their clubs. Zack dropped like a stone, unconscious, his face slamming into the sandy soil. Blood poured from his head, nose, and mouth.

While Zack was out, the Indians gathered up the screaming girls and what livestock and possessions they could, including Zack's shotgun, and prepared to ride away. The boy was dragging a goat toward the side of the house when the big man yelled at him.

"Mangas." The big Indian pointed at Zack and threw a long-bladed knife at the boy's feet. *"Termínalo. Ahora . . ."*

The boy, Mangas, reluctantly let the goat go and even more reluctantly picked up the knife.

"Why, Yellow Hawk?"

"Házlo, ahora." Yellow Hawk signed for Mangas to scalp Zack. "Do it, now."

Yellow Hawk and the others mounted up and began to move away. Mangas slowly approached Zack, who began to stir slightly, but was unable to rise. He opened his eyes and saw Mangas standing over him. The young Indian leaned down and grabbed him by the hair. Then with a shake of his head, he hit him with the handle of the knife instead of scalping him.

The sun was not quite up, and a light fog covered the desert floor like a dusty, low lying cloud. A grizzled frontiersman, riding west, rode his horse slowly up the wash below the Stephens farm. It was still, except for the slogging of the horse's hooves on the moist soil. The rider casually smoked a pipe as he rode through the quiet countryside. Suddenly, from the right, a blood-spattered goat bolted from the sand banks above the wash and dashed wildly in front of the man and his horse.

"What the . . . ?"

The man reined in his horse and watched

263

the goat race down the wash ahead of them and then dart into a thicket by the bank. He stood in the stirrups in an attempt to see over the bank to his left. In a moment, he sat back down in the saddle, but turned the horse left and they headed up and over the bank. On level ground, he could see the smoking remains of the Stephens house to his right. As he approached the house from the front, he spoke out loud, the horse his only audience.

"Slow. Go slow. Can't tell what's happened here yet."

He knocked the fire out of his pipe and pocketed it. He then slid off the horse, almost simultaneously removing a long-barreled rifle from its sheath alongside the horse's saddle. On the ground, he looped the reins around a nearby mesquite and checked to see that his rifle was loaded. He also checked for the large hunting knife he carried in his right boot.

He approached the house slowly, cautiously. At the door, he stood to one side for a moment, then quickly, ducked through. Inside, he waited for his eyes to adjust and saw that there was no danger within. At the back of the house, however, he saw the body of a grown woman.

"Aw, Lord. What have they done to you?"

He knelt beside the body.

The woman's clothes were torn nearly off and her body and face battered into a bloody mess. She was scalped. Sickened by the sight and smell, the man grimaced and stood.

"Must be more, this poor soul couldn't have been alone."

Rifle at the ready, he went outside and around to the right. The body of a man was near the back of the house. He knelt by it, observing the same brutal scene as with the woman. He picked up part of a broken war club and checked it over.

"Odd, that's Pima work. Must have been renegades, they don't usually. . . ."

He suddenly rose, cocked his head to one side, and hurried around behind the house. He found Zack, bashed, bloody and barely alive.

"Here, here, son. Don't try to move."

Zack managed to open his swollen, bloody eyes, tried to speak. The man knelt closer in order to hear.

"My . . . sister . . . find . . . help."

"What's that, son? Your sister? Don't worry now, just take 'er easy. We'll find your sister. I swear to you we will."

The Pueblito of Rio Seco, southwest of Gila

Bend, was so small the stage route from Tucson to Fort Yuma rumbled right by it without stopping. Barely a village at all, it was as barren and arid as its ironic name, Dry River, suggested. There were maybe half a dozen mud, wood, and adobe huts set back on either side of the sandy road leading into the village center.

Commercially, it consisted of a livery stable and blacksmith shop located at the northwest edge of town and, down the road on the east side, a general store. Directly across from the store was El Gato Negro cantina. Beyond town, to the southwest, a small Catholic church stood in silent opposition to the El Gato Negro and its hell-bent clientele.

A sharp, hot wind kicked up the loose topsoil of the village and slammed it against the sides of the church, the store and the cantina. Loud as that was, it was no match for the noise of El Gato Negro.

Inside the little cantina, notorious scalp hunter Captain Nathaniel "Nate" Wallace and about eight or nine of his men were holed up, drinking, gambling, fighting, whoring to their hearts' content. There are three past-their-prime Mexican prostitutes working the outlaws, a terrified two-man band banging out terrible music on a bad

266

guitar and worse trumpet, an equally terrified barkeep behind the bar, and an apparently mute Indian who swept a back corner of the filthy, dirty floor.

While his men shouted and caroused, Wallace, known among the Indians and Mexicans as *El Carnicero,* the Butcher, leaned with his back against the bar, one arm around the shoulders of the only attractive thing in the whole cantina, a very young Mexican girl named Luz Maria.

While Wallace drank and fondled the girl, his two main henchmen — Cross, a filthy man with rotten teeth and a scraggly beard, and the German, a short, relatively clean, but harsh man — counted out the gang's ill-gotten gains earned from killing and scalping Indians, Mexicans, or anyone with dark hair.

"Two hundred *pesos* for men, one hundred *pesos* for women and brats." The German eyed a stack of bills and coins in front of Cross. "Very kind of the Mexican government to be so generous." The men laughed. "What's the count, Cross?"

"I got fifteen hundred *pesos.*"

"Not a bad haul."

To amuse his fellow outlaws, the German turned and jammed a not quite empty bottle of whiskey into the playing end of the trumpet. The horn man leapt back in fear, his cut mouth bleeding slightly.

"*Ay, Díos mío, señor.*"

The outlaws guffawed. Cross pulled a huge hunting knife and jabbed it into the guitar. The guitarist held the instrument in front of himself like a shield. The horn man ran for the front door and was booted and slugged all the way out by the other outlaws. The guitarist tried to escape, too, but was hemmed in by Cross and the German.

"Play, boy, or die." Cross threatened.

"*No, señor, por favor.* Please."

Cross pulled his pistol and put it against the guitarist's temple. "Play."

Too frightened to stand, the man fell into a chair and fumbled with the guitar. The outlaws roared.

Across the room, Wallace pulled Luz Maria toward one of the back rooms of El Gato Negro. He swatted her on the butt as they disappeared. Cross watched the boss and weakly imitated him by grabbing one of the fat prostitutes and taking her into an adjoining room at the back of the bar.

The German grimaced in apparent disgust at the carnal debauchery. He then approached the bar, drew his pistol, and threatened to take his annoyance out on the barkeep. The man quickly produced a full bottle of whiskey to mollify the German, who grabbed the bottle and stalked out the front door.

Outside, the German climbed a short flight of steps up to the roof. On the rooftop was a sentry post of sorts with a short-backed wooden chair and small table. A dirty sheet with a large tear in one side had been rigged above as a canopy to battle the heat and bright desert sunshine. The German propped his feet on the table and lay his pistol on his lap. He leaned back and with a cursory look around the sun-whitened horizon began sipping his whiskey.

Whimpering, Luz Maria lay face down on a bed, naked, her back and buttocks red and scratched in several places. Wallace stood by the bed buttoning his pants. He reached into his pocket, pulled out a *peso,* and tossed it at the girl. The coin hit her on the back and she cried out. Wallace sat on the edge of the bed, grabbed her long, thick black hair and roughly pulled her to him.

"Did you like that, my little *puta*?"

Tears streamed down Luz Maria's face. *"Sí, señor."*

Wallace tightened his grip on her hair and forced a kiss on her bruised lips. "But did you love it, did you, my sweet?"

"Sí."

"Say it with meaning."

"I loved it, *señor,* please."

Wallace pushed the girl's head away and stood up. With a sardonic laugh, he slapped her sore butt and clomped out of the room. When he was safely gone, she mustered the courage to spit in his direction.

In the bar, things had quieted down considerably. Several outlaws were asleep or passed out, others quietly played cards. Cross stood by the bar with the wary barkeep. The other prostitutes, the guitar player, and the mute Indian had vacated the bar for safer havens.

Wallace walked into the room and leaned against the bar, surveying his dominion with the same sneer he had for the battered Luz Maria. For a few moments, he stood quietly at the bar, then suddenly his features changed. He became serious, alert. None of the others seemed to notice anything. Wallace turned to his left and signaled to Cross, then headed for the front door. Cross followed his boss outside onto the elevated wood walkway in front of El Gato Negro.

"What's up, Cap'n?"

"Where's the German?"

"Don't know. I was in back like you was till a few minutes ago."

270

Cross followed Wallace down a set of steps from the elevated sidewalk to the road. Wallace slowly walked out a few feet. Cross leaned back against the hitching post in front of the cantina. Wallace looked in all directions, his head up as if he were sniffing a scent like a trail dog.

"What do you hear, Cross?" Wallace spoke softly, projecting his voice directly at the other outlaw.

"I don't hear nothin'."

"Exactly."

Wallace looked up at the top of the cantina and spotted the German.

"German." He hissed.

The German looked down. Wallace pointed down the street, out of town to the southwest. The German moved cautiously and quietly, rose from his chair pistol in hand. He crouched down and peered off to his right toward the southwest part of town and the Catholic church.

From the roof, the German viewed the dusty grounds of the little church. There were a couple of Mesquite and Palo Verde trees by a small well and a tiny cemetery to one side of the church itself — and then, movement among the trees. One soldier appeared, then another, and more. The U. S. Cavalry, on foot, was making its way cautiously past the church toward the cantina and the outlaws. The German signaled to Wallace, crept to the edge of the building and descended the stairs.

"How many?" Wallace asked when the German had joined him and Cross in front of the cantina.

"Can't tell. Saw three, bound to be more. Cavalry."

Wallace signaled to the German that they were to get the horses out back and that Cross was to warn the other outlaws in the bar. Cross hurried off and Wallace and the German cautiously went behind the bar where the horses were tied up. They tried to act calmly, but over their shoulders they could see cavalrymen moving closer. With a crash that frightened both men and horses, Cross and the other outlaws came flying out the back door of the cantina. In a moment, the area was ablaze with gunfire.

With their ambush blown, the cavalry openly rushed the outlaws, firing black powder pistols and rifles at will. In the first volley, two of the outlaws were hit. One died by the back door, the other mortally wounded, but not yet dead, fell heavily into the horses and then under them. A couple of horses panicked and broke free, sending several outlaws scurrying after them.

Wallace, Cross and the German mounted and made a break toward the northwest, away from the cavalry, away from town. As they wheeled to ride off, they fired at the approaching cavalry with abandon. The closest two soldiers, one a tall thin trooper and the other still a boy, were shot dead.

With the heated outlaw opposition and the two soldiers killed, the rest of the troop slowed its assault and took cover. Their leader, a young lieutenant, tried to rally the troops, but was winged in the right shoulder for his efforts. He slumped to the ground, seeking protection behind a cottonwood stump. Cross and the German raced away to safety, but Wallace pulled up sixty or seventy yards from the attack and halted his horse.

Astride his mount, Wallace sneered as the survivors of his band managed to capture their loose horses, mount them and make a run from the scene. A brave soldier with a long barreled squirrel gun stepped out into the open by the cantina and picked off a final outlaw. Wallace took a rifle out of its sheath on the side of his horse, carefully aimed and with a thunderous explosion dropped the brave soldier dead in his tracks.

The young lieutenant clambered out from behind the tree stump and with pistol in hand called on his men to charge Wallace. Wallace sat calmly atop his horse, reloading the rifle. The lieutenant, followed at some distance by his men, fired his pistol again and again at Wallace, each round hitting closer and closer to the brazen outlaw.

Just as the lieutenant's rounds began to kick the dirt up around Wallace, the scalp hunter finished loading the rifle. With a foul smile, he lifted and aimed it at the lieutenant, who stopped still. Again, with a thunderous roar, Wallace discharged the rifle. The round hammered into the officer's forehead, penetrated the skull and exploded bloody brains out the back and onto the desert floor.

For a brief moment, before his body realized it was dead, the lieutenant remained upright, a strange, bewildered look on his face. Then he crumpled to the ground. His troops scurried off in all directions, seeking anything that would offer them protection from the deadly outlaw.

With a snort, Wallace turned his horse around and galloped toward the retreating figures of what remained of his band.

An early morning mist shrouded the banks of the Gila River and a Pima Indian village built along its shores. Life was just beginning to stir among the people. A few sleepy women wandered about starting fires or fetching water. A couple of old men also began to move around, and a chunky boy meandered along, yawning and looking for a place to relieve himself.

He started to urinate off the bank into the river but was scolded by one of the old women. The boy walked on out into the foggy desert in search of a good tree or bush. Finally, he located a thick mesquite, walked to the backside of it, away from the village and the bossy old women, and with a satisfied sigh urinated loudly and happily onto the desert floor.

He watched his stream steaming in the cool air, directing it back and forth over the ground. As the stream lessened, he looked up and saw, riding slowly out of the gloomy, misty air a group of mounted men. There were several warriors in the band and the boy saw that they also had two white girls with them. Behind them, an older man herded a small collection of ragged farm animals.

The boy quickly finished his business and with a squeal and a war whoop raced back to the village. In his headlong rush, he nearly ran over an old woman.

"Watch where you run, you great fat pig, you."

"They're back!" The boy raced on into the encampment. "They're back! Mangas and the others. They've got prisoners! White girl prisoners. Look! See!"

At the boy's persistent cries, the village turned out to see the raiding party return. Yellow Hawk and his band rode to the center of the village, where they stopped and dismounted. The village chief, a wizened old man with long gray hair, limped up to greet them.

"You have returned with animals for food, Yellow Hawk?"

"As you can see."

"They don't look like much."

"A little meat is better than no meat at all."

"Yes, you are right."

"We have war prisoners, as well." Dull eyes pulled Clara up for the chief to see.

"War prisoners? This girl? She's a warrior?"

"She is spoils."

"And the little one?"

"She's sickly." Yellow Hawk pointed to Janie. "She won't last."

"Why were they brought here?"

"For the bounty." Dull Eyes explained.

"What happened to your arm?"

"When we fought the whites, a boy did it to him," Yellow Hawk explained.

"He was a big boy," Dull Eyes avowed. "I killed him. Mangas cut his scalp, see?"

Mangas held up the scalps with some trepidation. Clara and Janie began to wail.

"What is the matter with them?" The startled chief looked at the girls. "We can't have all this yelling, it'll scare the women and children."

Dull Eyes threatened the girls with his good hand and their wails diminished to sobs and whimpers. Mangas used the opportunity to slink off.

"That's better." The chief smiled at the girls. "Take them to Light Hair, she'll know what to do with them."

"You're right." Yellow Hawk agreed.

"And you." The chief looked directly at Dull Eyes. "Go see the medicine man and get your arm fixed, it looks stupid dangling down like that. Stupider than your dull eyes."

"*Si, Jefe.*" Dull Eyes led the girls away. "I'll go now."

The chief motioned for Yellow Hawk to join him.

"Bringing those girls here is a mistake. It'll bring the horse soldiers down on us.

You must trade them right away."

"Trade them?" Yellow Hawk shrugged. "To who?"

"It doesn't matter. The Apaches. The Yavapai. Just get rid of them. Fast. The soldiers will kill all of us if they find those girls here."

"But they're worth. . . ."

"No. Do as I say. I have spoken."

"*Si, Jefe.* As you say."

In a rectangular box of a recovery room next to the medical dispensary at Fort Yuma, Zack Stephens lay on a bunk, the off-white sheets drenched from his sweat. His head was bandaged and there were ugly, crudely stitched up cuts on his face that a doctor examined.

"These stitches are looking better today. How are you feeling, young man? You've been through quite an ordeal I hear."

"All . . . right."

"You seem to be healing well." The doctor sat on the edge of the bed. "You'll be good as new soon."

"My head hurts and I can't feel some of my teeth."

"A natural reaction, son. Sometimes it seems like it has to get worse to get better. Before you know it, you'll be walking out of here strong and tall."

"I don't feel strong and tall. I feel like hell."

"There, there."

"I've got to find my sisters."

"Take it easy, son. You need to get well first."

Zack began to cry. "I couldn't save them."

"Now, now. Say, son, you've got a visitor today. Do you feel like seeing him?"

"Huh?"

"There's somebody waiting out here to see you. I expect you'll be glad to see him, too."

Zack looked at the door, wiped away his tears and propped himself up on one elbow.

The doctor walked to the door. "Come on in. He's able to see you now."

A tall, bearded, rather scruffy, pipe-smoking frontiersman walked into the room. Zack looked at the doctor.

"I don't. . . ."

"This is Irish Dan Parnell, Zack." The doctor explained. "This is the man who rescued you from the hostiles."

Parnell walked to the foot of Zack's bed, took off his hat, and stood there slowly puffing on his pipe.

The doctor sneezed and grimaced. "Do you have to smoke that foul-smelling thing

279

in here?"

The frontiersman removed his pipe with a smile and held it at his side, letting it go out on its own.

"Thank you, sir." Zack told Parnell. "For helping me . . . and my family."

"Was the least I could do." Parnell shuffled his feet.

"Has there been any word about my sisters, sir? Has anyone seen them?"

"Not that I know of, son. I never knowed they was took 'til a day or so ago. I thought it was just . . . just you was all that I found."

"Yes, sir. I'm beholden to you for that."

"It wasn't nothing to it. Anybody would have done the same for you."

The conversation waned and Parnell began to edge toward the door.

"I know they're alive, sir." Zack spoke quickly. "I heard them. I know the Indians took them."

"Easy, son." The doctor interjected. "Don't get yourself all worked up."

"Can you help me find them, Mister Parnell? Could you? You're a real frontiersman, you must know everything about being out here. Where they could have taken them and such."

"Son, you oughten not to think about it just yet. It's a hard thing and Indians are tough to figure. They could do anything. Go anywhere. Perhaps it would be best to trust in the Lord. It'll be his to decide."

"You won't help me?"

"Son. . . ."

"There's got to be somebody can. Ain't there, Doc?"

"Oh, there's someone can all right."

Zack lifted himself up in bed. "Who? Who?"

"I hesitate to say his name."

Parnell looked at the doctor. "It ain't who I'm thinking, I hope."

"Afraid so, Dan. Captain Nate Wallace is who I had in mind. None other."

Parnell shook his head. "Nate Wallace."

"Captain who?" Zack asked. "Who is he?"

"Only about the nastiest pole cat you can imagine, boy," Parnell said. "You don't want nothing to do with him and his kind."

"But if he can find my sisters. You said he could, Doc. You think he can?"

"Irish Dan is right, son. He is a terrible, dangerous man."

"I don't care. Where does he come from? Where is he?"

"From hell, boy." Parnell crossed himself. "He comes from hell. He kills Indians and Mexican women and children for money."

"They kill ours for nothing."

281

"All right, Zack, take it easy." The doctor tried to get him to lie down. "You'll make yourself worse again. You got to get well first."

"I'm going to get well, all right. And when I do, I'm going to get my sisters back. Even if it's the devil himself has to help me."

"If you fall in with him, son," Parnell warned Zack, "that's just what you'll be doing. 'Cause, by God, Nate Wallace is the devil himself."

Indian Agent Rafe Jones sat at a table in his small office poring over a stack of papers. The cluttered, dirty room was poorly lit by a flickering coal oil lamp. A .45 caliber derringer rested on the table beside him and he carried a hunting knife slid into his right boot.

Suddenly, but quietly, the front door to Jones' left opened and Captain Nate Wallace slipped quickly into the room. Jones was startled but quickly went for the derringer. In a heartbeat, Wallace had a cocked pistol nuzzle up against the side of Jones' head.

"You might ought to leave that little woman's gun where it lies."

"Wallace . . . what are you doing here?" Jones pulled his hand away from the derringer.

Wallace walked around behind Jones, keeping the pistol aimed at the shaking Indian Agent's head. He saw the hunting knife in Jones' boot and took it, holding it up in the sparse light to admire it.

"When did you start packin' one of these, Jones?"

"It's a dangerous place out here." Jones shuffled around in his seat, not looking at Wallace. "You know that better'n anybody."

Wallace nodded his agreement, then compared Jones' knife to his own, a huge, razor-sharp Bowie knife that he removed from an equally huge leather sheath worn on his belt.

"This is a dainty little thing, Jones." Wallace ran his knife suggestively across the agent's crotch. "Just right for servicing squaws, eh? That is what you do with them, ain't it? Slide the old steel in there?"

"What is it you want, Wallace? How did you get in the fort? Every man jack in the territory is after you. The law, the army, the Indians."

Wallace laughed.

"How did you?"

"That's my little secret. You don't need to concern yourself about it."

"Don't need . . . hell, Wallace, you've put me at risk coming here like this."

"You, you worthless possum face, at risk?" Wallace snorted. "There's a price on my head. A big one. They'd hang me if they caught me here. You at risk? Ha."

"All right, all right. Forget it. What do you want with me?"

"The usual."

"More dollars for pesos?" Jones grimaced. "Already?"

"Already."

"Why? A peso is the same as a dollar. They buy the same amount. They're exactly the same."

"Not to me. Not if you want to buy U.S. land. How can I become a rancher and settle down if I don't have plenty of this Godforsaken country for cattle to graze on?"

"How much this time?"

"Eighteen hundred."

"Eighteen hundred. My God, man." Jones looked up at Wallace, who shrugged. "How can I keep changing these for you? The bank will get suspicious."

"Tell them you're changing it for one of the tribes you . . . uh, help."

"I can't do it, Wallace. This is too much."

"Can't do it?" Wallace stepped menacingly toward the agent. "Can't do it? I suppose you forgot them two Indian girls I brought you?

Jones looked away. "There's no need. . . ."

"What happened to them, by the way? They disappear? Like the others? Maybe the government would like to know what you're up to. Maybe. . . ."

"Enough. Stop. I'll change the pesos. Please, stop."

"That's more like it." Wallace smiled.

"You'll get us all killed, Wallace, if you don't slow down."

"Ah, but there are so many scalps, and so little time."

Wallace leaned back and let out a hearty, loud laugh. Jones cringed and turned away.

Zack and Parnell rode slowly across the desert. Heat waves rose from the sandy soil in a false watery curtain, but there was no water near, and few signs of life. Small ground squirrels scurried about in the dry scrub as the horsemen passed by, but little else moved. High above and some distance ahead of the riders, high flying birds circled on thermals.

As they rode, Parnell filled his long-stemmed pipe, lit it, and puffed away contentedly. From time to time, he glanced over at the boy but said nothing. As they passed a cluster of prickly pear cacti, Zack, whose injuries had healed except for some bruises on his face and a cut on the side of his forehead still covered by a bandage, looked over at his riding partner.

"It seems so long ago."

Parnell took the pipe from his mouth. "What's that, lad? Long ago, you say?"

"My family . . . the Indians."

"Are you sure you want to remember all that, son?"

"It was good of the army to take care of everything. Don't you think, Mister Parnell?"

"Aye, I do, lad."

"I'm sure my ma and pa are happy now. They're in a good place. Isn't that right?"

"Well," Dan puffed on his pipe, "We can only hope so."

The two men rode on in silence for a spell, their horses clumping along slowly and methodically. As they cleared a small sand hill, in the near distance, they saw Zack's old house.

"Look, Mister Parnell." Zack pointed ahead. "There it is."

"And so it is. So it is."

In a matter of moments, they reached what was left of the Stephens spread. The house frame was relatively intact, but the roof and windows were gone. The white-washed exterior scorched in a number of places, providing stark testimony to the fire that gutted most of the interior.

They dismounted and cautiously approached the house. Inside they examined what was left of the once vital home. Little survived save the cookstove, some metal utensils and, oddly, a pair of women's shoes. Zack reached down and picked them up.

"My mother's."

Parnell patted the boy on the shoulder and pretended not to notice the tears in the young man's eyes.

"Could I have a few minutes, Mister Parnell?"

"I'll just be outside, lad."

"Thank you, sir."

Outside, Parnell checked on the horses and fiddled with their cinches and saddles. He looked out on the empty, barren, yet beautiful desert and up into the bright sky, but the birds that were circling there earlier have moved off. Filling his pipe and lighting it, he walked back to the house and along the side where Zack's father had been killed. He noticed several blackish red spots in the soil and quickly kicked sandy dirt over the stains to cover them.

He walked closer to the house and through

a knocked-out window saw Zack bent over, digging around behind what was left of the kitchen counter. The boy pulled something out and stood up. He turned slightly and Parnell could see what he had found. Zack held a leather money bag. It appeared bulky, full.

Parnell turned away from the window and slowly walked back to the front of the house. Zack exited what used to be the front door just as Parnell reached it. The pouch was nowhere to be seen, but Parnell noticed a considerable bulge in the left pocket of the boy's pants. Zack went straight to his horse and took the reins.

"I suppose I'm ready to go back now, Mister Parnell."

"Sure and you are, son. Well, let's be going then."

They mounted their horses and began to ride away, back toward the fort. They were still within sight of the house when Parnell turned in the saddle.

"I reckon you'll be using what you found back there to move on, eh, son?"

"You . . . you saw?"

"If it was me, I'd pull up stakes and head for California, maybe Oregon."

"Never. I can't leave without my sisters."

"What's done is done, lad. You'll be better

off putting it behind you."

"No, I won't. And I'll use what money I have to find them. All I need is a good scout who knows Indian ways. Someone like you, Mister Parnell."

"Oh, no, son. It's not my quarrel. I've lived peaceable with the Pima and the Yavapai, even the Apache, for many years."

"Not even for the money?" Zack reached into his pocket and held out the leather bag. "I've plenty here to pay you with, Mister Parnell. Please?"

"Save your money, Zack." Parnell held up his right hand. "You'll only come to grief if you keep on this course."

Zack puts the bag of money back in his pocket.

"I know my sisters are alive." Zack re-pocketed the bag. "I can feel it. And I'm going to get them back no matter what it takes."

With that, the boy spurred his mount into a fast trot and began to ride away. Parnell took off his hat and wiped the sweat from his forehead and face with a dirty old blue bandana. Sighing deeply, he swatted his horse with the reins and loped after Zack.

In an open air *ramada* in the center of the Pima Village, Clara Stephens in a dirty,

289

faded, torn dress, tried to give aid and comfort to her little sister Janie. She tended to her in a shaded corner of the ramada where a stick-covered roof provided the only shelter from the burning Arizona desert sun.

The younger girl, whose face flushed brightly, was deathly ill. She coughed repeatedly, spitting up blood. Clara wiped the blood away, but it was quickly replaced with each new cough. Behind Clara, two Indian boys watched with detachment except for an occasional comment in their own language.

"It's okay, honey," Clara assured her sister. "Clara's here. You'll be all right."

The little girl tried to speak but only managed to make a bloody bubble with her lips. Clara reached down and held her limp sister in her arms.

"Oh, God, please don't let her die. Please. Let someone find us, dear God. Help me."

While Clara spoke, an older Indian woman came up behind the native boys. Grabbing each one by the ear, she chased them away with a slap on their backsides. They ran off laughing.

"Vayanse! Vayan!" The woman yelled at the boys. "Get out of here! You nosey boys, go away."

When the boys were gone, the woman turned back toward Clara and Janie. She frowned at them. Clara saw the frown and burst out crying.

"Please help me. Help her. Help my sister. Oh, please."

The woman turned and walked away toward the chief's lodging. Inside, he reclined on a pallet of animal skins, resting with his eyes open. He didn't move when the woman barged in. She sat down opposite him on another pallet of animal skins and quietly stared at him.

"Yes, old woman." The chief spoke after a few moments of silence. "What is it that you want?"

"How could you not know what I want? What does everyone talk about these days? What's the only thing anyone can think about?"

The chief scratched his head but remained silent and calm.

"Well? You're the chief."

"Yes, and you are my wife. And then what?"

"You are as dimwitted as those fools who brought them."

"Oh, you mean the white girls."

"With this brain, you are chief?"

"With this wife, I am chief?"

291

"Your jokes won't do you any good. You have to answer me."

"Answer you what? Have you asked me a question?"

"You old coyote, you don't listen to me."

"Ask me something, then. I'll answer, or at least listen."

"Why did you let Yellow Hawk bring those white-eye girls here?"

"There was nothing to do. They brought them here. Yellow Hawk lives here. This is his home, too."

"You're getting too old. You would have stopped this before, but the men don't listen to you now. They don't respect you."

"So be it. So, what is the problem?"

"What is the problem? You don't see the problem?"

The chief shook his head.

"I'll tell you, then."

"There would be no way to stop you."

She glowered at the chief before speaking. "The young boys and men are ready to fight one another for the older white girl, and the small one is weak and dying."

"I have not seen this among the men and boys."

"You are blind."

"The little girl coughs a lot, but. . . ."

"But nothing, old man. She's dying right now."

"Right now?"

"Within one sun."

"That is bad."

"Bad? What do you think will happen when the white-eyes know the girl has died? The army soldiers will come. Or worse."

"Or worse? What worse?"

"The scalp hunters. The ones who slaughter us for money. It's all the excuse they would need."

The chief popped up off the floor like a man twenty years his junior.

"Do you think this is possible? That the scalp hunters will come?"

"I believe it."

The chief stood for a moment, rubbing his chin. When he spoke, it was as much to himself as to his wife.

"We must trade for the girls right away. To the Yavapai, or Apache. We can get several good ponies. We can. . . ."

"We can get them away from here, soon. Do you hear me, old man? Get rid of them now, right now."

"Yes." The chief looked his wife right in the eye. "We will get rid of them now."

Inside Fort Yuma, Zack, his facial injuries

almost healed, sat on the wooden walkway in front of a busy mercantile store. While people came and went behind him, he stared off into space. The fort was active with soldiers, frontiersmen, and Indian scouts.

Several riders entered the fort, and one of them, Agent Jones, tied up in front of the mercantile. He dismounted and started to walk past Zack, then stopped.

"How do, boy."

"Hello, sir." Zack slowly came out of his reverie.

"You're that boy's been running around with Dan Parnell, ain't you?"

"I do know Mister Parnell, yes, sir."

"Injuns got your sisters, did they?" Zack nodded. "Word is you been trying to round up help to go get them. That right?"

"Yes, sir."

"And they ain't been no takers?"

"No, sir."

"Where's Parnell?"

"He says he ain't got nothing against them Indians personal."

"A prudent course, for Parnell. Still I suppose you yourself is set on it."

"Oh, yes, sir. I will never let my sisters be kept by the Indians. I'll get them back no matter what it takes. Or costs."

"I can see you're hell bent for it. No matter what."

"Yes, sir."

"You have . . . uh, money?"

Zack reached inside his shirt and started to extract his stash of money. Jones quickly put a hand out to stop him.

"No, no. Not here, boy. Come with me back to my office. We can discuss the finances there. Perhaps, I know some people who can help you."

Zack rose and he and Jones walked toward the agent's office on the other side of the fort.

"Oh, yes, please, that's what I need, want, someone to help."

"It might not be cheap."

"I'm not rich, but I have some money."

"We can discuss that. I have contacts among the heathens. And with white men who do this sort of thing."

"I've heard of a Captain Wallace. Do you know him?"

Jones held a finger to his lips to silence Zack.

"Maybe he can help?" Zack whispered as they reached the office.

"If you have enough money." Jones opened the door.

"Wallace is your man. He will get your

sisters back."

"I'll do whatever I have to."

"Step on into my office and we'll see what we can do."

"Thank you, sir. I'm obliged to you."

"Think nothing of it, boy. Think nothing of it."

They went inside Jones' office and he closed the door behind them.

Wallace and his men holed up in a hotel used as a way station for pilgrims being ferried across the Colorado River to the promise of gold and a better life in California. The hotel was a clean, well-lighted place, filled with a mix of hopeful, expectant travelers, and rough-edged locals.

Wallace, Cross, and the German sat at a table in the restaurant. Two chunky waitresses hustled meals, glasses of tea, and slices of apple pie to the motley clientele. The room was lit by a series of strategically placed coal oil lamps. As Wallace and his two main men were served their dessert of huge pieces of apple pie, Jones and Zack entered. The German nudged Wallace who casually looked over then turned back to his pie.

Jones, with Zack hanging back a bit, approached the outlaws' table. They stopped behind the empty seat across the table from the German. Jones waited for Wallace to finish a bite of apple pie before speaking.

"Evening, Captain. Gentlemen."

Cross glowered at the new arrivals. The German grunted. Wallace took another bite of pie.

"Uh . . . uh, this, uh, young man here is Mister Zachary Stephens." Jones pressed on. "Perhaps you've heard of him. It was his family's unfortunate lot to be attacked by a group of hostiles some time back."

"Yeah, we heard of him." Cross gruffly interrupted. "So what?"

"Well . . . gentlemen, the boy lost his mother and father. . . ."

"Touching." Cross snorted.

"He lost his parents and believes his sisters were carried off by the savages."

"Believes they were carried off?" The German laughed.

"The poor boy was left for dead himself. But he's sure his sisters are alive."

"And how would he know that?"

"I can feel them." Zack stepped forward. "I know they're alive. Sometimes it feels weaker, but I know they're still alive. I know it."

Wallace calmly finished his pie, set the fork on the plate and pushed it toward the center of the table.

"Oh, they're alive all right." He belched. "Least ways they was."

"Have you seen them?" Zack could barely control his excitement. "Do you know where they are? Oh, thank God, thank God. I knew it."

"Hold your horses, boy. I just said I heard something about it, that's all. There's no reason to get all in a lather yet."

"Yes, sir. But —"

"But nothing. You got any idea what you're up against? These things ain't easy. We're dealing with heathens here. If they have your sisters, they won't give them up for free."

"I — I have money. Tell them, Mister Jones. You. . . ."

"I've been helping the poor lad since his tragic story first became known to me." Jones interrupted. "And right away, I said, Zack, my boy, Captain Nate Wallace is our man. If anyone can find the girls, it'll be Captain Wallace. You bet you."

Wallace shook his head and laughed. Cross and the German exchanged looks that mingled disgust and lack of respect for the Indian agent.

"Well, as I was saying to the boy, Captain Wallace and his band of courageous frontiersmen are our best bet in a difficult spot like this. Working together, we. . . ."

Wallace lifted his left hand with the index finger raised.

"I believe we can take care of it from here, Mister Jones. I'm sure you have important business to attend to at the agency."

"But — very well. Young Zachary, I will leave you in the capable hands of Captain Wallace."

Jones bowed slightly and backed away from the table. The German aimed his finger at the agent like he was going to shoot him. Cross laughed loudly, revealing a set of scraggly, filthy teeth. When Jones was gone, Wallace addressed Zack directly.

"Have a seat, boy."

Zack sat in an empty chair to Wallace's left, but the German spoke first.

"What is it you think we can do for you, boy?"

"I've got to have help to find my sisters, sir. I don't know where else to turn."

Wallace looked at Zack. "Why would we want to get mixed up in something like this, boy?"

"People say you're not afraid of the Indians. That you hunt them."

Cross suddenly reached out and grabbed

Zack by the collar. "Who told you such a thing?"

At a minute nod from Wallace, Cross released the boy, who tried to regain his composure.

"Everyone at Fort Yuma says it, sir."

"And right they are, too."

Cross and the German laughed. Wallace cut off the laughter with a slight motion of his right hand.

"Me and my men have been known to exact retribution from the savages when it was needed. But why would we do it for you? The red bastards steal white women all the time. They don't usually last long either."

"But — I know they're still alive. They just have to be."

"You been out here long, son?" Wallace's tone softened somewhat.

"A year or so, sir."

"Then you must see how these things go. Still, perhaps there's a remedy. But it may be a steep one, if you get my meaning."

Zack slowly understood the outlaw's meaning and he reached inside his shirt to extract the money pouch. The German reached across the table to stop the boy from bringing the money out in public, but it was nearly out by then. Just as the pouch cleared cloth, Cross ripped it from Zack's hands and hurriedly lowered it out of sight beneath the table.

"Hey, give that back."

Cross quickly pulled a hunting knife and put the long, sharp blade alongside Zack's left temple. The boy froze in place. Wallace moved quickly to cut off the scene, as several nearby patrons began to take notice of the outlaws' table. Wallace smiled as if it were all a game and motioned for Cross to lower the knife, then he signaled for Cross to hand over the money.

"There, there, gentlemen. Settle down. No need to get all riled up over nothing. We're a peaceable group, now, aren't we? As for you, boy, take this money back and forget you came here tonight. And forget your sisters. We know about these things and word has been around about your sisters. They've been with the Indians too long. You'd be wasting your time. Now go on, get out."

Cross and the German moved to "escort" Zack out.

"Please, Captain Wallace, you've got to help me. You're my last chance. You can have all my money if you'll just help me."

Cross and the German stood Zack up.

"All of it, eh?"

"If you let me go along with you."

Cross snorted and the German laughed.

"Not likely, boy." Wallace waved his right hand.

Cross and the German grabbed Zack, took him outside and unceremoniously dumped him on the wooden plank front porch. When the outlaws went back inside, Zack sat on the top step of the stairs with his head in his hands. After a moment or so, the outlaws came out of the hotel, clumping by Zack, their spurs jingling, and walked down the steps to the road.

Impulsively, Zack leapt up and followed. As the outlaws reached an alley separating the hotel from a nearby blacksmith's shop, Wallace walking several feet ahead, Cross and the German suddenly turned, grabbed Zack and pulled him into the dark alleyway.

In a heartbeat Cross hammered several punches into Zack's solar plexus and the boy collapsed, breathless and in agony, to his knees. While Cross hovered over him, the German reached inside his shirt and removed the money pouch.

"You won't be needing this anymore, boy."

"Damn you, you bastards." Zack cried out, coughing and spitting. "I'll get you someday."

For his trouble, the outlaws slapped Zack

on the back of the head and gave him a sharp kick in the side. After Cross and the German left the alley, Zack tried to lift himself up. As he did, Wallace suddenly appeared in front of him. Light from a room in the hotel shone across the outlaw's face giving it a devilish cast. He took several dollar coins from the pouch he had taken from his henchmen and threw them at the boy.

"A word to the wise, son, forget all about this. And forget about your women folks. For the last time, be on your way. This country ain't for the likes of you. Go on back to where you come from. Leave this country to men. It ain't no place for a boy."

Zack glared at Wallace, but the anger and hate in his expression were lost in the darkness of the night. His only response to the outlaw was a pain racked cough followed by loud retching. Wallace plodded off into the night.

In the middle of a hot morning that promised to get far hotter, Irish Dan Parnell led a pack horse on a rope behind his own mount. He was at the edge of a Pima Village that bustled with activity as the people seemed to be loading up their gear and belongings.

Besides a few barking dogs and some playful children, no one took notice of the visitor until he reached midway in the village. Finally, the old village chief emerged from a flat roofed home and spied Parnell. The old man slowly made his way over to the Irishman.

"*Buenos dias, Irlandes.* It has been a long time. We are honored by your visit."

"The same to you, *jefe.* It is I who am honored to be here."

"Do you need water? Food? Please join us if you do."

"Thank you, chief, no. I have both in plenty. Your kindness is appreciated."

"You are always welcome here, Irish. Our home is your home."

"My thanks again, *jefe.*

"Have you brought things to trade?"

"Yes, sir. I have tobacco and flour. And other things."

"That is good, but you can see we are busy today and have little time for trading."

"With no disrespect, Chief, it looks like the whole village is moving. Has something happened?"

"Nothing bad, no." The chief dissembled, answering slowly and not looking Parnell in the eye. "But the game gets more scarce each day and the fish are fewer in the river. The many new white people who come, with no disrespect to you, Irish, take up the land we need. We must leave to find a better place. With more food and more land. That is why we go."

"I have something for you, *jefe.*" Parnell dismounted. "Something to make your journey more pleasurable."

He walked back to the pack horse and after digging around in a sack slung over the animal, brought out a couple of small cloth bags. He walked back to the chief and handed them to the old man.

"What is this, Irish?"

"Both are tobacco, chief, one for chewing, the other for your long pipes."

"Wait here, Irish." The chief grinned happily and held the bags aloft like they were trophies. "I have something for you, too."

Before Parnell could make a mild protest, the Chief hurried off to his home leaving the Irishman alone in the center of the village.

Parnell took the opportunity to look around. Other than the general movement, he saw nothing until, at the far end of the village by the river, he spotted a small elevated dirt mound and, by the mound, a colorful piece of cloth.

He took a step in that direction, but just then the old chief emerged from his house, closely followed by his wife. They hurried to Parnell's side. The chief extended his right hand. In it, he held an intricately carved, long wooden pipe.

"For you, Irish. As our friend."

"For me? I am much honored, great *jefe*. My thanks and respect to you."

"For you, to take now and go." The chief's wife frowned at Parnell. The chief gave her a stern look which she ignored.

"Yes, thank you. I must be going on."

"It is a good day to travel." The woman pointed toward the desert.

"Don't be rude, old woman. You will offend our guest."

"No, no. I have to go now. I'm looking for someone."

"Looking . . . for someone?" The chief and his wife exchanged a quick glance.

"Yes, maybe you heard, two white girls were taken from near the fort. One little, one older."

"Hmmm." The chief scratched his chin and puzzled over the news.

"No." His wife quickly answered. "We haven't heard. Not around here."

"No? I thought it would be spoken of everywhere. Well, perhaps not."

"No, Irish, we haven't heard of such a thing. There are many bad men around nowadays."

"These were renegades who did it. That I'm sure of."

"Too many renegades these days." The chief's wife agreed. "They can't be controlled. There are too many. White ones, too."

"Yes, there are renegade whites, too. You are right." Parnell took the rope from the pack horse and remounted his horse. "Goodbye, my friends. I hope we will see each other in your new home."

"We hope so as well, Irish." The chief raised a hand in goodbye.

"Goodbye." Parnell doffed his hat.

"Until next time."

"Until next time."

Parnell slowly rode away. At the outskirts of the village, he looked back. The chief and his wife had gone back inside, so he headed his horse toward the elevated dirt mound he had seen before. As he neared it he saw, stuck between the ears of a huge, gnarled prickly pear plant, the shiny cloth he'd spotted earlier. Riding close to the plant, Parnell reached out and snagged the piece of cloth.

Yellow Hawk, Dull Eyes, and Mangas took Clara Stephens from the Pima village to a Yavapai village to trade her. The girl was dirty, unkempt and scared wild looking. She sat on a broken-down pony led on a rope by Yellow Hawk. Mangas held the shotgun he took during the attack on the Stephens family.

As the small party slowly entered the center of the village, they followed a horse trodden path that ran through the middle of a dozen or so Yavapai homes which resembled the loose canopy and pole construction of the Apache wickiup. The Yavapai turned out to see who the unexpected visitors were. Their chief and several warriors met the group in mid-village.

"How are you, big chief?" Yellow Hawk spoke. "I bring greetings from the Pima people."

"Welcome, Yellow Hawk. It has been a long time since we have seen you."

"Life is hard. Time is short."

"*Si, es.* And greetings, Dull Eyes, and the young boy."

"This is Mangas." Yellow Hawk explained, "Soon to be a great warrior. He has cut the hair of many white eyes." The Yavapai all looked over at Mangas, who averted his eyes.

"Welcome to you as well, young Mangas. Our home is your home."

"*Gracias, jefe.*" Mangas nodded. "I am

honored."

After the greetings were over, the Yavapai gravitated to Clara, who sat without expression on her horse. The Yavapai moved around her. The chief and a couple of warriors reached out to touch her which caused her to flinch. After a moment or two the Yavapai pulled back and spoke again to the Pima.

"You captured this one?" The chief asked.

"Yes, *jefe.*" Yellow Hawk shook his head. "In a fierce battle. We defeated the white eyes and took this girl as a trophy."

Mangas moved as if he would speak out but when he saw the Yavapai notice him, he again averted his eyes and said nothing.

"The Pima are brave fighters." One of the Yavapai warriors declared. "The girl is a good trophy."

"That is true," Dull Eyes agreed. "But we have no more use for her."

"Our people move farther along the Gila," Yellow Hawk added. "We must join them soon."

"You are saying the girl is for trade?" The chief asked.

"All things are for trade."

The Yavapai buzzed among themselves for a moment. Down the village, directly in Mangas' line of sight, Jones the Indian agent appeared with a group of Yavapai women. The agent carried several items and loaded them into his saddle bags and mounted his horse. For a moment, he looked back, and he and Mangas stared at each other. Then Jones noticed the other Yavapai and Pima, and Clara Stephens. With no outward indication of interest, Jones turned his horse and rode out of the village. Yellow Hawk saw.

"That was Jones, the agent?"

"Yes, he trades with us often," the chief said.

"I distrust him."

"All distrust him."

Yellow Hawk grunted, and he, Dull Eyes, and Mangas dismounted. Leading the girl's horse, they walked toward a large open-air structure that served as the Yavapai communal gathering place.

"Chief, this white girl is strong. Worth a lot."

"I trust your word, Yellow Hawk, but she is trouble."

"The white eye agent saw her." Mangas noted.

"You would be wise to let her go or trade her elsewhere."

"You are . . . not interested in trading this day?" Yellow Hawk held his hands palms upward.

"Oh, yes, my friend. We have much to trade, but not for the girl. She is bad luck, I feel."

"We should kill her and let the coyotes eat her bones."

"Calm yourself, Dull Eyes, we can trade her on the other side of the river. In California."

"Yes, perhaps." The chief shook his head. "But for now, please accept our hospitality. Stay with us. We will eat and drink and find other things to trade. We have new rifles and shells."

"From the white eye agent."

"Yes, young Mangas, you are very perceptive. I can see you will be a great warrior someday."

"I do not trust the agent. He has no heart or soul."

"Well said. But he is gone now. His trading done. Please join us. Welcome, my friends."

The two groups of warriors gathered inside the *ramada* to eat, drink, and talk. Mangas grabbed a large piece of meat and a piece of *tortilla* and stood near Clara Stephens, who was now surrounded by curious Yavapai women and children, watching the horizon toward which the agent, Jones, had ridden.

Zack Stephens sat with his head in his hands in a back room off the Fort Yuma doctor's quarters. He had been there since the attack of Wallace's men and the doctor had let him stay to recover. After a few moments, he rose and paced around the room, then sat down again just as the doctor knocked and entered the room.

"How are we doin' today, son?" Zack was silent. "There, there, boy. All is not lost. There's someone here to see you."

"I don't want to see anyone. Not anyone."

"Come on now, buck up. It is a tough world out here. You've got to be strong, lad."

"What for? I can't do anything. No one will help me, no one. . . ."

Zack's complaint was suddenly shut off by the unannounced, boot clumping arrival of Dan Parnell.

"Maybe I can help you now, Zack."

"Irish Dan." Zack looked at the frontiersman in disbelief.

"Parnell," the doctor laughed, "you have an amazing knack for showing up when I least expect you."

"All the better to keep you on your toes, sawbones."

"Where have you been, Mister Parnell?" Zack stood. "I never thought you'd come back."

"Doctor, could I have a moment alone with the boy?"

"Certainly, Mister Parnell, I can see you need to talk. I understand. Zack, if you need anything, just holler."

"Thanks, Doc."

"I'll be just out here should anyone need me, Mister Parnell."

"Appreciate it, doctor."

"You have good news, Mister Parnell?" Zack asked, after the doctor was gone. "I surely hope so."

"It's hard to say, son. Maybe some bad, maybe some good."

"What do you mean?"

"I've just come from the Pima village over on the Gila. . . ."

"Was there word of my sisters? Was there?"

"Take it easy." Parnell held up his hand. "Not exactly. No word as such. The Pima were packing up to get out. Moving their whole village on up the Gila."

"I don't understand."

"Well, that means something big is or has been up. I didn't see any white girls with them, but they were mighty fidgety when I sort of asked what was going on."

"You think they have my sisters?"

"No, I don't. But I believe they may know something about them."

"Let's go, then. Let's go to the Pima and demand they help us get them back."

"That wouldn't be a good idea. They'll be far away by now. No use." Zack hung his head. "One thing, though, I have to ask you, son."

Zack looked up at Parnell. "What?"

"Do you recollect what your sisters was wearing the day of the attack?"

"Same as always, I reckon. Some kind of gingham dresses. Different colors, I suppose."

"Would you recognize a piece of one of them?"

"Reckon I might."

Parnell produced the piece of cloth he found on the cactus at the Pima village. Zack's eyes widened.

"This is Janie's dress. My little sister. Where'd you get it?"

"Found it at the Pima village. Near one end of town."

"And?"

"And it was by a small, new grave."

Zack was silent for a moment. He rubbed the back of his neck.

"Take me to that grave, please. You said

314

the Pima were leaving. I want to see for myself."

"It's too late now, today, and besides, there was no sign of the older girl. If we intend to save her, we need to get ready and head out in the morning. If the hunch I'm feeling is right, we'll know the fate of both your sisters soon enough."

"What do you know, Mister Parnell? What do you mean?"

"I just got this sixth sense about it. It may be a dangerous gamble. This whole thing is beginning to smell of Nate Wallace and Jones, the agent. And if Jones is in it, then the Yavapai may be in it, too. We could walk into something nasty, son. Are you up to it?"

"I want the Indians that took my sisters to pay, and I got a personal thing against Wallace and his damned German and gang."

"Well, if I'm on the right track, I got a good idea where they'll be. We'll head out before first light. You game?"

"I'm game enough. Just show me where we're going."

"All right, then, we'll do it."

The sun was not yet fully up, but the clear sky was bright over the quiet Yavapai village. A light breeze rustled through the

Mesquite and the Palo Verde, gently moving the few wisps of smoke remaining from late lit fires. It was so still and tranquil in the village that not even the dogs were straying about and the ponies' heads were hung in restful slumber.

Beneath the open air ramada, Yellow Hawk, Dull Eyes, and Mangas slept soundly, weapons lying carelessly around them. The white girl, Clara Stephens, was nowhere to be seen. A rooster crowed and an awakening horse snorted.

Inside a Yavapai house midway in the village, Clara Stephens stirred. Huddled in a threadbare, dusty blanket, she was with three other women, all Yavapai. Nearest her was a plump teenage girl who slept soundly, on her left a woman of perhaps thirty years who tossed and turned. Directly across was an older woman, who yawned revealing several missing front teeth. Though sleepy, she was vigilant and kept a sharp eye on Clara. When Clara saw the older woman watching her, she rolled away and hid her head.

Outside, the quiet village was bathed in the rays of the now fully risen sun. Some life began to stir, and a young boy padded out of his house and urinated in the bushes nearby. As he turned to go back inside, a

316

horse whinnied, then another and several others began to move about, their hooves stamping on the dusty, desert ground. The boy lifted his head and listened. He sniffed the air. A dog barked.

There was a slight rumble audible, almost like thunder from a far distant storm, but the rumble grew louder, increased again. The boy stepped out into the pathway through the village and lifted his left hand above his eyes to block out the blinding rays of the sun. Suddenly, the noise intensified, and it was clearly the sound of horses, many horses, riding out of the sun toward the Yavapai village. Turning so fast that he fell, the boy raced back through the village yelling at the top of his lungs.

"Riders! Horses! Wake up! Horses! Riders!"

He rushed down the village pathway toward the ramada where the Pima slept. The village began to awaken, and people moved about in their houses. The sound of the incoming riders came closer and closer to the village. The boy continued crying out and raced up breathlessly to the Pima in the ramada. The first to react was Dull Eyes, who rose up brandishing a rifle. The boy skidded to a stop as Yellow Hawk and Mangas also leapt up.

"What is it?" Yellow Hawk grabbed the little boy. "Why are you yelling?"

"Riders . . . coming . . . now!"

Yellow Hawk pushed the boy to one side with his rifle. The three Pima squinted into the blinding eastern sky. As they did, the approaching riders broke into the village, guns blazing.

The Yavapai, now aware of the danger, rushed outside. Women scurried in every direction with children, sleepy-eyed men hurried about brandishing weapons, but the attackers, Captain Nate Wallace and his brigands, had the advantage of surprise and fire power. They roared through the village shooting down anything that moved . . . men, women, children. It was indiscriminate slaughter.

In moments, the riders reached the ramada and with amazing ease shot down Yellow Hawk and Dull Eyes who fell lifeless, their bodies riddled with outlaw bullets. Mangas, firing Zack's stolen shotgun, put up strong resistance even as the Yavapai chief and several of his main warriors fell. Weaving around in front and back of burning houses, Mangas picked off two or three of the outlaws.

But the cause was lost. Wallace's vicious band, having wiped out the majority of the

318

men in the first wave of death, began to systematically kill every living being in the village. They spared no one and no thing. Dogs, horses, chickens, all were killed.

Mangas found a dirt hill and hid behind it. He watched as Wallace went from house to house until at last the outlaw leader found the one with Clara Stephens in it. Wallace drug the girl out, simultaneously fighting off the older Yavapai woman who had watched over the white girl. When the woman kept fighting, Wallace shot her dead and then did the same to the other two women who ran crying out of the house.

Mangas leapt up from his hiding place and fired at Wallace but was too far away for the buckshot to do any harm. As Mangas fumbled to reload the shotgun, the German appeared by Wallace's side. The German took careful aim with a long barrel pistol and fired at Mangas. The shot hit the young Pima in the left side of his chest and knocked him backwards over the round hill and out of sight.

In the village, with most of the Yavapai dead or dying, the outlaws brandished scalping knives. Some of them helped Wallace throw Clara Stephens up onto a horse while the main group began moving through the village to begin the ghastly taking of scalps. Screams of agony blended with the smoke and dust filling the air above the burning village.

Some three or four miles from the Yavapai village, Parnell and Zack rode around the side of a small hill and up onto a rise. Parnell immediately held up his hand to stop Zack.

"What? What is it, Mister Parnell?"

"Listen."

In the silence they could hear the clear report of gunfire cracking in the early morning air.

"Damn it, just as I feared."

"What?"

"It's Wallace. He got here first."

"Come on, then. Hurry."

Zack reared in the saddle to spur his horse on, but Parnell reached out and stopped him.

"No."

"But there's no time to waste. Clara could be in there."

"Listen, lad." Parnell continued to hold back the boy's mount. "We'll ride fast but not at a gallop. We have to keep our wits about us. When we get near, if it is Wallace's men, follow my lead. And keep a cool head, no matter what you see. You understand?"

"Yes, sir. I understand."

"Then let's go."

The two men spurred their horses and rode toward the sound of diminishing gunfire, dust kicking up from behind.

When Zack and Parnell reached the vicinity of the Yavapai village, they reined in their horses, dismounted and took up defensive positions behind a rocky sand hill overlooking the village. Below them, they watched the final stages of the outlaw slaughter of the Yavapai. Smoke rose from the burnt shells of several houses. Animals and humans lay all around, dead and mutilated. Among the carnage walked several of Wallace's outlaws, left behind to complete the foul task of scalping every last victim.

Even from this distance, the scene was horrid enough to cause Zack to lower his head. Suddenly, Parnell tapped him on the shoulder. The boy slowly raised his head to see the Irishman pointing to their left, in a westerly direction. Zack looked out to see a cloud of dust close to the ground in the distance. The cloud was diminishing, indicative of movement away from their position.

"Wallace?" he asked Parnell.

"Wallace."

"Let's go after him."

"We will. But first we take care of these filthy bastards."

"How?"

"You go around to the east on our right, I'll come around the other end of the village. Keep your wits about you, boy, don't shoot me."

Zack nodded and Parnell moved off to the left. Zack made his way around to the east end of the village, the direction from which the original attack came. He moved carefully, slipping behind a large prickly pear and then a tall, thick saguaro.

At the very end of the burned-out village, he hid behind the wall of a partially standing adobe house. Ahead and to his right, he saw the immobile, prone body of Mangas. To his left, moving toward the sand hill behind which Mangas lay, two outlaws slowly walked through the rubble, bloody knives in hand.

"I think I seen another one over here somewhere." The taller of the two men spoke.

His partner pointed at the sand hill ahead of them. "I'll check over this hill."

"Hurry up, we gotta catch up to the others."

"Go on, get the horses. I'll be right there."

The tall outlaw walked away then, back

toward the center of the village. His partner continued looking for more bodies to scalp. Zack watched his every move. After a few moments the outlaw reached the sand hill behind which Mangas lay. The young Pima crawled backwards on his stomach, very slowly, down the hill toward the banks of the river. When the outlaw cleared the top of the hill, Mangas immediately stopped moving and played dead, but too late. The outlaw pulled a pistol he had tucked behind his belt.

"I knew it, you little bastard. Playing dead on me, were you?"

Mangas rose to his knees and pulled a knife. The outlaw drew a bead on him. Suddenly, there was the powerful report of a rifle and the surprised outlaw, mortally wounded in the chest, turned to see Zack standing across the scrub land from him, smoke curling from his rifle barrel. The outlaw fell to the ground dead.

Mangas and Zack exchanged looks of mutual recognition, but had no time to size each other up as the tall outlaw had quickly reacted to the shooting. He ran toward his fallen comrade.

"I see you, boy, you're gonna die."

Zack broke eye contact with Mangas to face the new threat. As he did, two loud shots rang out from the other end of the village. The tall outlaw stopped his advance and for a moment looked toward the sound of the shots. When he turned back to face Zack, the boy's rifle was trained on him. The outlaw raised his weapon, but before he could get it chest high, Zack squeezed off a booming, echoing round. The shot hit the outlaw square in the forehead, a red hole appearing between the eyes, midway up the skull. For seconds, he wavered in that zone between life and death, then the lifeless form crumpled and fell backward onto the ground.

As soon as he realized he was no longer in immediate danger, Zack turned toward where he had last seen Mangas, but the young Indian was gone. Cautiously, slowly, Zack made his way to where the young Pima had lain. When there, he kicked the first outlaw with his boot and pushed him over to check his face. The man, blood still running from the wound to his heart, was definitely dead. Zack reached down and took his rifle and pistol, tucking the six-shooter behind his own belt.

Climbing back to the top of the sand hill, Zack surveyed the area below him toward the river. He saw no sign of Mangas. Then, for just a moment, there was movement near the edge of the river, a horse, an Indian pony, moved slowly along the bank.

He squinted to see if there was anyone hanging on to the horse, but at that distance he couldn't tell at first. Then, an extra leg appeared behind the horse, a human leg. He raised his rifle to fire, but paused and leaped down behind the hill. Rifle at the ready he watched a rider approaching. Peering over the edge of the hill, he saw it was Dan Parnell and he was leading Zack's horse.

"Zack, boy, where are you, lad?"

Zack leaped up from behind the hill, causing Parnell to draw down on him, ready to fire. He froze in place and Parnell caught himself in time. The Irishman uncocked his pistol and shook his head.

"Damn, boy, I nearly shot you."

"Irish Dan, Irish Dan. We did it. We got 'em."

"Aye, that we did, lad. But we've got a hell of a row yet to hoe. Saddle up, boy, there's a hard ride ahead of us."

Zack mounted his horse, rifle in hand, and they headed back westward through the devastated village. They passed the dead mutilated bodies of innumerable Yavapai.

"What filth this Wallace and his band are." Dan spat on the ground. "All these people

325

dead. Scalped. Poor buggers. All dead."

They passed the bodies of Yellow Hawk and Dull Eyes lying beneath the charred remains of the ramada. They were scalped, their clothes covered in their own blood.

"Those two there, boy. That's Yellow Hawk and Dull Eyes, the ones who took your sisters."

"Yes."

"The Lord will judge them now. They've paid with their own death. Everyone is dead."

They contemplated the massacre for a few minutes more, then spurred their horses to a trot and rode out of the ruin that was, only hours before, a vital, living Yavapai village.

Settled against the back wall of a small canyon, the Wallace gang's hideout consisted of two wooden cabins, one larger than the other, facing each other across the rocky desert floor. Coming into the Saguaro, mesquite and prickly pear-filled canyon, the larger of the two cabins was on the left. The smaller on the right.

Two outlaws stood guard at the entrance to the canyon. One was up on a large boulder near the front passage watching for intruders. The second was further back toward the cabins. He sat on a dead saguaro smoking.

The canyon appeared to be a dead end, but at its very back a barely visible horse trail offered an escape route for the outlaws. This trail was monitored by another guard, who leaned against a corral containing most of the outlaws' horses. Fresh mounts were tied up in front of the large cabin.

Despite recent events, the outlaw hideaway seemed calm, even tranquil. All was quiet, save for a light rustling of the wind through the mesquite and desert scrub. Smoke curled from a small chimney pipe coming out of the roof of the larger cabin.

Inside that sparsely furnished cabin, Clara Stephens worked over a hot wood stove that sat in a far corner of the room. She was cooking a stew and trying to make biscuits with the meager supplies provided.

Wallace, Cross, and the German were at a small table boisterously counting up the bounty from their recent raid on the Yavapai. On the table before them was a pile of black-haired scalps and two bottles of whiskey from which they frequently drank.

"It's a good take, a damned good one." Cross sat one of the whiskey bottles down. "But not as good as we did that time down by Ajo."

"Here's another adult male." The German lifted a scalp and dropped it back down on the pile. "Another one hundred *pesos.*"

"To the government of Sonora." Cross raised his bottle of whiskey.

Wallace poured himself a large drink from the other bottle into a dirty water glass, then handed the bottle to the German. The three men toasted their ill-gotten gain.

"It's going to be over five thousand," the German estimated.

"Piddling wages." Wallace snorted.

"Not like back in '39, ey, Captain?" Cross laughed

Wallace grunted and poured more whiskey in his glass.

"What was '39?" the German asked.

"We made a killing, so to speak. Must have brought in $50,000 that year. Remember, captain?

"More like $60,000."

"$60,000." The German whistled.

"That was the year Captain Wallace seen the Mexicans couldn't tell the difference between their own people's scalps and the scalps of the blasted Indians. We really cleaned up then, didn't we?"

"Cleaned up the whole damn territory almost." Wallace and Cross guffawed. The German nodded approvingly.

As the laughter subsided, Clara brought over the pot of stew. Wallace swept the scalps onto the floor and the girl began ladling out big portions of the foul looking concoction into large wooden bowls.

As she worked, Wallace began to take notice of the girl. He took in the shape of her breasts and hips underneath her dirty dress. She tried to ignore him, but he reached out and played with the folds of her dress. Impulsively, he pulled her to him.

"Come here, girl."

"No. Stop."

He forced her, resisting, to sit on his lap. He held her roughly and forced a kiss on her.

"Please don't."

Wallace continued manhandling the girl until she slapped him hard in the face. Surprised, he let her go for a moment and she leaped up. Cross grabbed her from behind and Wallace rose as if to strike her. She cowered beneath his raised fist, but then he seemed to lose interest and sat back down. He signaled to Cross to release her.

"Let her go."

"If you don't want her, boss. I'll take her."

"I said, let her go."

Cross reluctantly released the girl, who

hurried back to the relative safety of the stove.

"Get us some bread, girl." Wallace ordered. "German, hand me that bottle of whiskey."

The German reached the bottle over to Wallace, who poured himself another big drink. Weeping silently, Clara pulled the biscuits from the stove oven and prepared to serve them to the men. Sullen and quieter now, the outlaws continued hammering down the whiskey.

As he had when they approached the Yavapai village, Parnell found higher ground for he and Zack to scout the area before deciding on a plan of action. They saw the two guards at the front of the canyon, the cabins, and the guard back by the horse corral. Zack had moved up next to Parnell when the frontiersman signaled him to stay down. He put a finger to his lips, and they watched as a rider suddenly appeared at the head of the canyon. The guards waved the man in.

"It's the agent, Jones," Zack whispered.

"Curse his filthy hide."

They watched Jones salute the guards then ride on to the large cabin where he hitched his horse alongside the three mounts in front. He hopped down and hurried into the main cabin.

Inside the main outlaw cabin, Wallace, Cross, and the German were devouring stew and biscuits. They ate sloppily, their beards and mustaches full of stew pieces and biscuit crumbs. Suddenly, the front door opened, and Jones entered. In a heartbeat he was greeted by three drawn .44 caliber pistols, all aimed right at his chest. He stopped in his tracks.

"P— please, don't shoot." He stuttered, both hands raised high. "I'm here to warn you."

"You bloody fool, Jones." The German slowly lowered his weapon.

"I could blow your damn head right off, Indian trader." Cross brought his pistol down as well.

"And I ought to let him do it." Wallace did not lower his pistol. "Do something like that again, and I will."

"Sorry, captain, but I came to warn you. You know me, I always do right by you."

"Shee-it." Cross laughed.

"So, warn me."

"It's that meddlesome doctor. The one back at the Fort." Jones looked across the room, noticing Clara for the first time,

331

Cross saw.

"What's the matter? Never seen a white woman before, squaw man?"

Jones stared at Clara, but she lowered her head to avoid his gaze, then turned and faced the stove.

"So, what has the doctor done?" Wallace waved his pistol at Jones.

"Somehow," Jones tore himself away from looking at the girl, "they got wind of the Yavapai, uh, situation back at the fort. Now, that busybody doctor got them all riled up about it and that girl there. They say they're coming after you."

"The damn cavalry." Cross blew out a deep breath. "Whew."

"Yes, the cavalry. And anyone else that old sawbones could muster. Vigilantes. They want your hide, Wallace."

"Lot of people want my hide."

"I say we head straight for Mexico." The German proposed.

"You afraid of the army, German?"

"Don't you understand. It's not just the army coming. Indians, whoever hates you all."

"The army couldn't whup their own mother," Cross declared. "I say we stand and fight."

"It's a large force. Civilians, too. They

may. . . ."

"Shut up, Jones." Wallace rose from his chair. "All of you, shut up. It'll take them a good day or more to track us. No reason to panic. Cross, send a couple of boys out as scouts. We'll get ready here and then head out in the morning."

"I could go with them." Jones edged toward the door.

"You stay here with me." Wallace motioned for him to sit. "I want to see where you're at." Jones sulked but made no effort to leave.

Wallace signaled to Cross who headed for the door. "Send one of those idiots that let our Indian Agent friend in so easily."

"Yes, sir, boss."

From their overlook of the outlaw camp, Parnell and Zack saw Cross come out of the larger cabin and go into the smaller one. He shortly emerged again followed by two other outlaws.

"Something's up," Parnell pointed. "Look."

Down below, Cross gesticulated, and he and the two men grabbed the three horses in front of the larger cabin and led them up to where the two guards were at the entrance to the hideout. Cross motioned to the first guard and then the guard and the two other men mounted the horses and rode out of the camp. Cross spoke with the remaining guard for a moment then headed back to the larger cabin.

When Cross reentered the cabin, Parnell backed down the hill to his horse. He reached in his saddlebag and came up with two sticks of dynamite. He made his way back to Zack's side.

"What's that for, Mister Parnell. What are you fixing to do?"

"There's no telling how many of those varmints are in that little cabin. I aim to blow 'em out of there."

"What if my sister's in there?"

"No way. She's in the big one with Wallace and his cronies. She's too valuable to him, he won't let her out of his sight."

"What about the two guards left?"

"The one at the back by the corral has done dropped off. He's asleep, the fool."

"How do we do it?"

Parnell pulled a large hunting knife from his belt and ran it along under his own chin as if slitting a throat. Zack gulped. Parnell handed the boy the big knife.

"Wha— what about you?"

Parnell pulled up his pant leg to reveal another knife in his boot.

"This will be the tough part, son, but we've got to get rid of the two guards. Then we blow the little cabin and I figure Wallace and his two confederates will come out at the explosion. We ambush them then."

"I don't know. I never cut nobody's throat before."

"You've got to, lad. We have to surprise them if we want to get your sister back. You can do it." Zack looked doubtfully at the long, wide-bladed knife in his hands. "You take sleeping beauty back there. I'll get the other one up front. Be ready to shoot when the explosions come. We'll only have one chance with Wallace. He's twice as mean as a rattlesnake and harder to catch and hold."

"Okay."

"Good luck, boy."

"Y— yeah."

Parnell moved off to the left, away from Zack who slowly and reluctantly worked his way down the hill towards the back of the camp.

Because the rear guard was asleep, he was easy to sneak up on. But that was little help to the indecisive Zack. He made several tentative steps toward the guard, but each time pulled back. Finally, his nerves got the better of him and he lost his grip on the knife. It fell to the ground, banging loudly

335

off a rock. The guard awakened, slowly at first, eyes barely opening, then he realized what was up and he leaped to his feet brandishing a rifle.

In a panic, Zack went for his pistol and managed to drag it out and aim it at the guard. For a moment they both stood still, weapons trained on each other. Then, to the surprise of each, Zack's gun discharged. The round hit the man directly in the heart. For a moment, he remained upright, shocked, then he fell backward onto the rocks, dead. Dumbfounded, Zack stared at the motionless outlaw. Then, without warning there was a tremendous roar as the first stick of Parnell's dynamite went off back at the small cabin.

"Oh, my." Zack leaped into action, raced toward the outlaw cabins. Just then the second stick of dynamite blew. "Dear Lord, help me."

At the sound of Zack's pistol going off at the back of the camp, the outlaws inside the main cabin had jumped up, grabbed weapons and taken up defensive positions behind wood covered windows. As they did, the first stick of Parnell's dynamite went off causing general confusion. They jumped back and forth from window to window and then the second stick of dynamite exploded.

"Help me, Oh, Jesus, help me." The agent, Jones, cried out in terror. "It's the army. We'll all be killed."

He made a beeline for the front door, hell bent to escape. Clara also tried to run, but Cross quickly grabbed and held her, leaving Wallace and the German to deal with Jones and the unseen attackers beyond the cabin.

The agent made it to the front door and rushed out, but he only got a few feet before the German reached the doorway with pistol drawn. He fired twice, both rounds hitting Jones in the back, and the agent fell face first, dead on the ground. The German had little time to savor his kill, however, as pistol shots rang out and wood chips from the door flew around his head. He sprang back into the building, slamming the door shut behind.

"How many of them are there?" Wallace cried out.

"Couldn't tell. At least two, three, maybe more."

On the other side of the room, Cross continued struggling with Clara. "What do we do with this damn girl?"

"Tie her up," Wallace told him. "She's worth too much to leave."

"We ought to kill her anyway."

"Shut up and do what I tell you."

337

Wallace grabbed a length of rope from a nearby table and tossed it to Cross. Just then, the door burst open and a mortally wounded outlaw staggered in burnt badly and bleeding. Clara used this moment of confusion to make her break.

She kicked Cross hard in the groin, doubling him up, and then ran out the front door. The wounded outlaw fell dead on the floor and a limping Cross, the German and Wallace made for a large wooden window at the back of the cabin.

Cross swung the window open and was face to face with Irish Dan Parnell who instantly fired twice. One bullet hit the outlaw squarely in the chest, the other went right through his left eye. Cross fell dead, his body hanging half in, half out of the cabin.

The German appeared in the window behind the slumped body of Cross and Parnell raised his pistol again but was too slow. The German shot first, hitting Parnell in the left shoulder. The round spun the frontiersman around. Despite his wound he fired several shots back at the cabin, missing the outlaws but coming close enough to chase them back.

Inside the cabin, chaos fully reined.

"Come on, German." Wallace yelled as he

ran toward the front door.

"After you, Captain."

"Come on you foreign bastard."

"Go easy, we don't know how many of them are out there."

"If it's that damn girl's brother, I'll kill and scalp the little son-of-a-bitch."

"Getting out alive is all that matters."

Recklessly they burst out of the cabin, pistols drawn but directly into Zack's line of fire. Clara was behind him and he shielded her with his body.

"Get away, sister! Run!" He raised his pistol.

Clara scrambled off as Zack aimed his pistol and fired quickly. One round nicked Wallace high on the left thigh and he twisted away in pain. He fell against the German causing his shot to miss Zack, and in the collision he dropped his own pistol. Zack fired again and hit the German solidly in the chest, knocking him flat. He then took aim at Wallace who searched for his pistol. Unable to find it, the outlaw drew a huge hunting knife from his belt and rushed forward madly. Zack pulled the trigger again but the pistol misfired.

In the blink of an eye, Wallace was on the boy, knocking the pistol out of his hand and seizing him roughly. With a powerful backhand motion, he knocked Zack to the ground, semi-conscious. Clara, who had watched her brother's struggle, charged Wallace. She hit and scratched him, but he quickly and roughly subdued her.

"Your brother and your pretty hair's gonna be all mine, little girlie." Wallace laughed.

With a sharp punch, he knocked Clara out. She fell beside her brother who, staggering and fuzzy headed, tried to stand. Wallace lifted him by his hair and held the hunting knife aloft, its sharp blade nearing Zack's scalp.

At that moment, the wounded Parnell came around the corner of the cabin. He drew a bead on Wallace but just as he did, from the rolling smoke of the burning, smaller outlaw cabin, Mangas suddenly emerged like an apparition of bloody, vengeful death.

The outlaw pushed Zack away and turned to face the new threats. With a wild cry, Mangas fired the shotgun, buckshot ripping into Wallace's chest. The outlaw stumbled back and dropped his knife. From instinct he reached for his pistol, but his holster was empty. Mangas fired the second barrel flush into the outlaw's body. Wallace fell to the ground, dead at last.

For a long moment, the three remaining men, Zack, Parnell, and Mangas, looked at each other in silent amazement. Clara scurried back to Zack's side and held onto him tightly. Then Mangas held up Zack's shotgun in a gesture of shared recognition and triumph.

"Zack." Clara tried to get her still dazed brother to understand. "That's one of them. He's one of the Indians that stole me and killed Momma and Daddy . . . and Janie."

Parnell aimed his pistol at Mangas.

"No, wait." Zack cried. "He just saved my life. *Our* lives, Clara. He was with the others, but he's different, different than them."

Parnell lowered his pistol and Zack signaled to Mangas with an upraised hand, palm outward. Manges shook the shotgun in the air, then tossed it over toward Zack.

At that moment, the group simultaneously turned toward the front of the canyon. With the thunderous sound of hooves hitting the ground, a cavalry detachment rode in. At their head was the Fort Yuma doctor. With them, in custody, were the three outlaw scouts that had left the hideout earlier.

The detachment came to a halt in front of Zack and the others. Parnell picked up movement to his right, turned and looked for Mangas, but the young Indian had vanished — disappeared behind the smoke and rubble of the smaller outlaw cabin. The doctor and a young captain dismounted and approached. The doctor quickly set in checking the injuries of the survivors, Clara first.

"Let me take a look at you, young lady."

He gave Clara a cursory examination and smiled benevolently.

"No worse for the wear, considering what you've been through. You're a strong, and lucky, young woman. This galoot here just wouldn't give up on you, you know?"

"Yes, sir, I knew he wouldn't."

"And you, Zack Stephens, another bop on that noggin of yours, boy, and you're going to be addled." Zack tried to laugh. "You'll be fine, son, both of you will with some rest. We'll get you back to the fort and you'll be all right again in no time."

Finally, the doctor checked Parnell's gunshot wound.

"Looks like you got lucky, too, as luck goes, Mister Parnell. Bullet went right through you. We'll bandage you for now and I'll fix you up good as new back at the fort."

He began applying a temporary bandage to Parnell's wound.

"Easy there, Doc. It still smarts."

"Sir," the captain addressed Parnell, "one

of our lead scouts tells me he saw a hostile near here. A young warrior, probably one of those involved in kidnapping the young lady here."

"Well —"

"No, sir," Zack interjected. "Your scout must have been mistaken. The ones that took my sister were all killed with the Yavapai in their village. There weren't no survivors. Saw their bodies myself."

Parnell and Clara exchanged looks as did the doctor and the captain. There was a silent pause.

"Perhaps you're right." The captain finally spoke. "The scout must have seen someone else."

"Yes, captain." Parnell nodded. "I'm sure that's it. Your man saw someone else."

The captain tapped the front of his hat with two fingers in a casual salute. The doctor finished with Parnell's temporary bandage and then he and the captain moved off, rejoining the detachment.

"Well, miss," the frontiersman said when the three of them were alone. "This is quite a brother you have here. He never once gave up on finding you."

"You done everything, Dan, er, Mister Parnell."

"I'm so grateful to you, Mister Parnell,

and to my brother."

"Maybe we'll go on to California now, Clara, like you always talked about."

"Do you mean it, Zack?" Clara hugged him. "Could we? Oh, yes, I want to now more than ever."

"Would you come with us, Mister Parnell." Zack and Clara looked hopefully at the weather-beaten face of the frontiersman.

"Yes, please do." Clara smiled happily.

Parnell shuffled his feet, then looked down. "That's mighty nice of you young folk to invite me and all, but. . . ."

"But?" Zack asked.

"I reckon I'll be stayin' on here in the territory. This is my place, my country. This is where I belong."

Parnell motioned for Zack and Clara to walk ahead and join the waiting doctor and the captain who held horses ready for them to ride.

"Well, sir." Zack reached out his hand which the frontiersman shook. "If you ever change your mind."

"Much obliged, son. Now let's saddle up. We got a fair piece to go yet."

"Yes, sir, we surely do."

The group mounted their horses and rode off toward Fort Yuma and into the unseen but now hopeful future.

ABOUT THE AUTHORS

Dusty Richards grew up riding horses and watching his western heroes on the big screen. He even wrote book reports for his classmates, making up westerns since English teachers didn't read that kind of book. His mother, though, didn't want him to be a cowboy, so he went to college, then worked for Tyson Foods and auctioned cattle when he wasn't an anchor on television. His lifelong dream, though, was to write the novels he loved. He sat on the stoop of Zane Grey's cabin and promised he'd one day get published, as well. In 1992, that promise became a reality when his first book, *Noble's Way,* hit the shelves. In the years since, he's published over 160 more, winning nearly every major award for western literature along the way. His 150th novel, *The Mustanger and the Lady,* was adapted for the silver screen and released as the motion picture *Painted Woman* in 2017.

In a review for the movie, *True West* magazine proclaimed Dusty "the greatest living western fiction writer alive." Sadly, Dusty passed away in early 2018, leaving behind a legion of fans and a legacy of great western writing that will live on for generations.

J.B. Hogan is a prolific and award-winning author. He grew up in Fayetteville, Arkansas, but moved to Southern California in 1961 before entering the U. S. Air Force in 1964. After the military, he went back to college, receiving a Ph.D. in English from Arizona State University in 1979. J.B. has published over 250 stories and poems. His novels, *The Apostate, Living Behind Time, Losing Cotton,* and *Tin Hollow* — as well as his local baseball history book, *Angels in the Ozarks,* a short story collection entitled *Fallen,* and his book of poetry, *The Rubicon* — are available at Amazon, iBooks, Barnes & Noble, Books-A-Million, and Walmart. When he's not writing or teaching, J.B. plays upright bass in East of Zion, a family band specializing in bluegrass-flavored Americana music, and is active in the Washington County (AR) Historical Society, where he's recently served as President.

The employees of Thorndike Press hope you have enjoyed this Large Print book. All our Thorndike Large Print titles are designed for easy reading, and all our books are made to last. Other Thorndike Press Large Print books are available at your library, through selected bookstores, or directly from us.

For information about titles, please call:
(800) 223-1244

or visit our website at:
gale.com/thorndike

Printed in the USA
CPSIA information can be obtained
at www.ICGtesting.com
JSHW020204271124
74329JS00003B/3